LIF

CHRISTOPHER MORVANT
BASED ON HIS ORIGINAL SCREENPLAY

also includes
NIGHT DRIVE
based on his short film

Encyclopocalypse Publications
www.encyclopocalypse.com

Life Cycle
Copyright © 2024 by Christopher Morvant

Night Drive
Copyright © 2024 by Christopher Morvant

All Rights Reserved.

First Edition
ISBN: 978-1-960721-66-2

Original Poster Designed by Matthew Dix
Cover Layout by Sean Duregger
Interior design and formatting by Sean Duregger
Edited by Mark Alan Miller

The characters and events in this book are fictitious. Any similarity to real persons, living, dead or undead is coincidental and not intended by the author.

No part of this book may be reproduced in any form or by any electronic or mechanical means, including information storage and retrieval systems, without permission in writing from the publisher, except by a reviewer who may quote brief passages in a review.

CONTENTS

LIFE CYCLE

The Novelization	7
Film Notes	99
Image Gallery	103

NIGHT DRIVE

The Short Story	119
Film Notes	129
Image Gallery	133
About the Author	139

It was an honor to work alongside so many creative and talented individuals. They toiled tirelessly to make "Life Cycle" a reality and allowed me to focus all of my attention on my true passion: coffee and donuts. I look forward to watching the film they helped me create once I have completed my work with the macchiato and maple bar menace. They tell me that it has something to do with computers, I really think those will be the wave of the future.

Christopher Morvant
2024

README

I've finally finished writing this abominable book. Is it a true story? They tell me it was just a movie... It couldn't have just been a movie. I was there, inside. I remember the bits and fragments, vivid jigsaw pieces in my mind that just won't fit.

But none of that matters. All that matters is that despite my best efforts, my torment persists. It has been mandated that I introduce this collection of incoherent ramblings. Is there no end to this torture?

I've been trapped here for months, surrounded by four concrete walls.

On the wall behind me is embedded a heavy steel door. I've tried bashing various parts of my anatomy against it: feet, hands, head, but to no avail. It has a small portion that can be slid open, presumably to spy on an inmate. But I don't believe that they will open that again, not after what I sent through it last time.

On the wall to my left is positioned a mirror such that it perfectly frames a reflection of my head. My own face incessantly studies me from the corner of my eyes. I've learned to despise that accusing visage.

On the wall to my right someone has crudely etched an indecent limerick. All right, I admit it was me. My own vain attempt to be remembered; a few trashy words that might enjoy a lifespan longer than my own.

On the final wall hangs the only decoration: a calendar, a cat calendar, each month adorned with what I can only assume is meant to be an adorable image. Don't they know I'm allergic to cats? Just looking at those furry little monsters causes my throat to swell.

Back to the point: who or what am I?

I'm a pile of rotting flesh propped up in front of a Underwood typewriter. I had a computer once but they took it from me, punishment for a single game of minesweeper. If I don't expose the hidden dangers, who will?

No more spell check, no more delete, and the backspace key is next to useless since they took my white out. I wasn't sniffing it, I just like the smell. Every error means another brutalizing round of paper alignment, exposing my bare flesh to the treacherous machinery.

My fingers are already raw from endless hours of pounding keys. The unceasing mechanical click-clack is driving me mad, telling you about it only doubles the effect. Mad, maybe that's the whole point.

The few hours they allow me for sleep are filled with the screams of other trapped souls. Or were those screams my own? I can't tell the difference anymore.

I just received my daily visit from a large bald brute whom I call Meatball. He probably told me his name at some point, I didn't bother to remember. He looks like a Meatball.

Meatball wears a green jumpsuit covered in front by a blood-stained white rubber apron. He has a puffy flap of flesh for a mouth, sausages for fingers. I know the feel of those fat meaty fingers wrapped around my neck too well.

Tucked in his apron is a black marker which he uses to draw a large 'X' on the calendar in honor of the demise of another day. He breathes heavily as he rubs the squeaky marker along each slow careful line.

I can't resist teasing the beast. "Only 25 letters left to learn and I'll teach you to spell your name, Meatball."

The sausages squeeze into a fist, the facial flesh flap into a grin. He swings a crooked arm in my direction. I hear the flat sound of meat slapping against more meat. The pain shoots all the way to my feet and then my body goes numb for an instant. Dead silence. Suddenly the feeling returns, a jolt of electricity lighting up my extremities, it's exhilarating, the smack of cold water in your face. I'm still alive, you son of a bitch.

As he leaves me in beautiful agony he turns from the door, "More coffee, Mr. Morvant?"

"You're damn right more coffee!"

I feel good now, relatively. Let's finish this thing and then, maybe, they'll finally let me die.

Read on at your own peril, and make of it what you will.

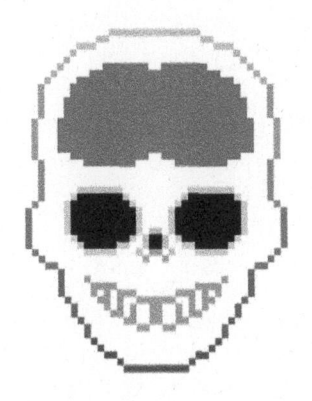

LIFE CYCLE
THE NOVELIZATION

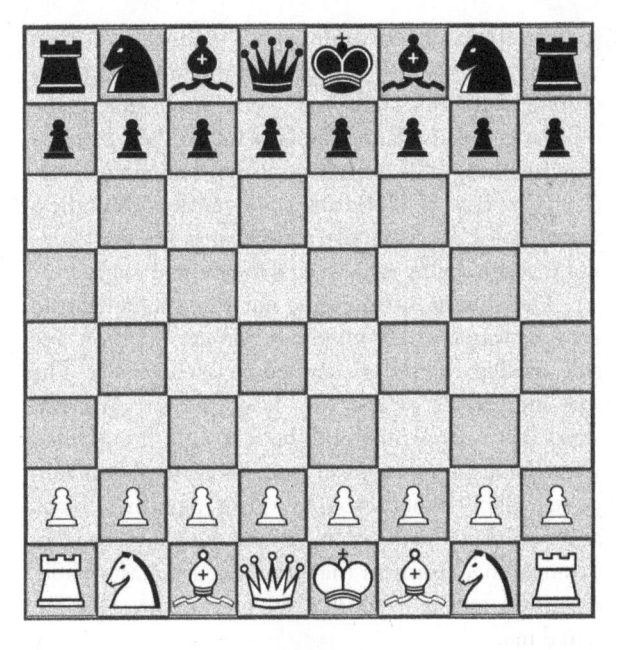

11001

I sat staring at my creation. We had been down similar paths countless times, slowly improving with each, but always a seeming infinity from my goal... our goal.

This time was different though, the training wheels were off. I could no longer let my flaws, my insecurities corrupt the experimental space. There's a fun irony in there, my humanity being the bug in the code. Imagine that, me too human.

I was on a low-back gray velvet rolling chair in front of a rather plain wooden desk, the usual leg-cave bordered by mahogany drawers, something out of some 70s catalog: 'streamlined utility for the discriminating home office.' On top were a couple of monochrome monitors circa 1983, one apple green, the other a gorgeous Baltic amber. I found their cathode glow soothing, a beautiful simplicity that allowed creativity instead of cluttering one's mind with endless visual noise. It absolutely complicated my workflow, but that's probably what I liked the most about it.

The volume surrounding me was a subterranean rumpus room, a few windows perched high on one side, walled in by dark stained wooden panels. The sole method of escape was a set of avocado green stairs that wrapped behind the rear wall. It was filled with the accumulations of decades of forgotten zeitgeists: globe liquor cabinet, velvet paintings, black and white 10" television, mustard yellow couch... Strange anachronisms that frightened me as a child, disgusted me as a youth, and now endlessly fascinated me.

Perched on the end of the desk in front of me was my aforementioned creation, the culmination of the prior 3 years of my life: an animatronic head. Naturally it had the basic operational control: pitch, roll, yaw, along with the expected facial movements: eyes, eyelids, mouth. In addition to these I had painstakingly crafted servo driven facial articulation allowing a variety of human-like expressions. It could smile, frown, scowl, pout, etc. My earlier efforts, consisting of varied 2d and 3d computer renderings, felt empty, like a bad 90s horror movie. My experiment needed something concrete, visceral, like a bad 80s horror movie.

At this point you most likely are demanding to know why I had gone to such great lengths, what possible motive could warrant such toil? Patience, dear reader, I entreat you. I spent several years in the creation of this story, allow me a few pages to let it unfold.

Having been sitting for several hours I decided to stand for a moment to stretch my numb legs. This dry run would most likely crash quickly and I would be thrust once again into the debugging process, digging through piles of code well into the morning.

Turning from the desk, I paced slowly towards my sleeping cubicle, a small raised back room (doorless) probably intended to securely contain one or two small children while the adults lounged in front. It was now cluttered with the forgotten possessions of dead generations which poured out from an open closet and left only enough room for me to lay. The visible patch of carpet on which I slept was a bright blue pond that flowed like a river down a few steps into the main room where it drained into a large circular maroon rug, a lake of blood on which I now stood.

My mental chaos was peaking, that confused combination of excitement and dread, possibility in conflict with probability. I turned to face my creation and spoke with forced confidence, "Cherry..."

This was the name I had chosen for my digital assistant, the secretarial specter which controlled an assortment of menial electronic tasks and was always available, day or night, at the tip of my tongue. Perhaps the moniker Igor would have proved more apt, but I have a fondness for the more feminine digitized voice, especially one donning a British accent. Also, being a fan of sci-fi schlock, the short lived (on screen but not in my memories) suds-soaked titular robotress seemed a fitting namesake for my electronic companion. Needless to say, using her name tickled me in a spot Igor couldn't reach.

"Cherry, verbal authorization code 237. Verify base expansion 11703-1."

She replied succinctly, "Expansion verified."

I stared intently at the inanimate head-shaped pile of plastic in front of me. Nothing. I addressed it, "Can you hear me?"

No response... This was the base level, only a thin layer of randomization at this point. Delays should be at a minimum. Perhaps the processing power of the CPU was under too much strain already or maybe I didn't tighten one of the connections adequately. I could see no obvious problems on the diagnostics panel emanating from my monitor.

Growing impatient, I tried clapping my hands together, an often overlooked scientific approach. Moving down my mental checklist of suggested debugging techniques, I was considering the efficacy of kicking the desk.

I repeated myself instead, "Can you hear me?"

Suddenly I sensed the spark of life ignite inside the dormant head, the slight sounds of servos awakening. I could feel it's eyes looking at me, then through me, then at me again, struggling to focus. My mechanized marionette was coming to life.

LIFE CYCLE

Its mouth began to open, an electric surge shooting through my body as it spoke, "What is this?"

"Life!" I replied, barely able to contain my excitement. I had heard that voice emanating from that mouth many times but this was unique. These were Its first words , independent of scripting or prompting. It was as though my own voice was being spoken by another.

It was a cognizant question as well, I might consider the same query were I in such a position. Even if next it sputtered out random noises and caught fire, it would still have been a resounding success.

"What am I?" the head continued. This was either a profound introspection or a complete failure of programming.

"You don't know?" I prodded.

"I exist, but have no memory of existing. I can speak, but have no memory of learning to speak. I know that learning is the means by which one acquires knowledge. Yet I have knowledge without having learned it."

Do I need to tell you how pleased with myself I was at this point?

"I gave you that knowledge, I built you, I created you."

I sat in my chair, a Cheshire grin plastered to my face.

"I've given you a base level of intelligence, speech comprehension, visual pattern recognition, and problem solving, along with video, audio and data memory. Just enough fertile soil from which to grow."

"And what are you?" the head inquired.

"Call me Carl."

You may call me Carl as well, dear reader. Your patience has paid off, your narrator has a name, and I have delivered to you the information required without the need to repeat myself. Although I did waste a considerable amount of your time explaining that fact, for me it was an ideal opportunity to boast, time well spent.

The head gazed around the room for a moment until it found its reflection in an old shaving mirror which I had suspended alongside it. My rationale? The ability for it to formulate facial expressions independently required its ability to see its own face at some point.

"And who are you?" the head inquired of this heretofore unfamiliar face.

I had no expectation that the reflection would offer an answer, so I responded instead, "That is you, your reflection."

"So this is me. I will have to remember that." It gazed at the mirror enamored with its reflected visage.

I continued enthusiastically, "You're basically an empty slate, your own Tabula Rasa. You have the ability to alter your mental functions by creating new expansions: subroutine arrangements which access all of your input/output functionality. Before integration each expansion must be authorized..."

"Must be authorized verbally by you."

I was a bit taken aback by the interruption.

It turned to look at me, "I know this already, it is a part of my core knowledge base. What I do not know is my goal. What is my purpose? Why do I exist?"

LIFE CYCLE

The surreal nature of the situation suddenly overcame me. I was having an unscripted conversation with a disembodied robotic head. I caught myself, focused my attention and forged on.

"I'm getting to that, retreading the familiar in order to reach the new. I wanted to reveal your purpose to you face to face. I wanted it to be real and personal, not just a line of code."

"And?"

My excitement grew again as I answered, "You are to become human."

"Am I human?"

Not quite the response I was anticipating.

"No. You're a robot."

"So you want me to impersonate a human?"

"No, more than that. To distill the mental essence of a human being."

We were back on track.

"I want you to be a near perfect human simulation. To think and respond as a human would, not just reproduce the results. So that we might better understand what it is to be human and whether or not that can be recreated with microchips."

"So I am to learn what it is to be human, and implement that within myself. Understood."

"You have all the resources of the Internet at your virtual fingertips."

I was delighted to have progressed this far into the experiment. All of the basic operations were functioning together as designed. Despite excessive testing of them in isolation, there is always a distinct probability of some unforeseen interference.

My creation returned its gaze to the mirror and studied its features. "Why did you give me this anthropomorphic face?"

I was well prepared for this question having asked it of myself several times.

"Partially so that you could express yourself physically. There's a lot to being human that requires some level of physicality. Secondly, so that you might have an identity. You can look in that mirror and know you're seeing yourself. And finally, for myself, to be able to interact with you in a real space."

Seemingly satisfied with my response, the head broke its gaze with the mirror to peer down at a chess table. Once again, I purposefully declined to describe the table or even mention its existence previously because this seemed a more apt spot to do so.

The chess table sat beside the desk, directly below the head. It was at my right side and could be manipulated by me while at the desk, though it was much more comfortable to roll my chair around it to the proper position. It was composed of a chessboard inlaid on a square mahogany table top which had an inset drawer on one side. It was supported by an elegant column that dropped into a pedestal base. The handcrafted wooden pieces were prepared in all of their proper opening positions, the black pieces in front of the peering animatronic, the white pieces standing ready for myself.

I decided to anticipate my creation's curiosity, "Up until now, you've been my chess partner... opponent. It's how I tested your basic functionality before properly bringing you into existence. In fact, your un-

LIFE CYCLE

derlying code began as a humble program I created to play chess with, but I began to wonder what I was capable of..."

"Shall we play a game?" the head turned to look me square in the eyes.

"Do you want to?"

"As of now, I do not have the capability to want."

"Well then let's play. Why not?"

The idea of this game intrigued me. How would my creation's progress affect his ability? How would it affect my own?

It returned its gaze to the chessboard, mine followed.

"You still have all your chess learning intact. I was too lazy to remove it."

"It's your move, Carl."

"Naturally."

Be forewarned dear reader: my animatronic marvel will speak his moves aloud and I, being a gracious host, will move his pieces accordingly. For your edification and to close the gaps in our game, I will let you know, in painful detail, every move I made. If these gory details do not fascinate you, let them flow in one eye and out the other and be assured that it is a legitimate chess match which will ensue intermittently throughout my story. Any similarity to famous historical chess matches is purely coincidental.

I opened with knight to F3, starting out slowly and not committing too much too soon.

The head spoke without hesitation, "Knight to F6." It seemed that my opponent would be equally cautious. I moved the piece.

Just knowing that the wheels were turning behind those blue eyes weighed on my nerves. Was it judging my move, my hesitation, am I blinking too much? Too little?

It seemed better to speak than to overthink, "I'm sorry to have to tell you, but you were never able to beat me."

I moved pawn to C4, clearing the way for my cavalry.

"Pawn to G6." The head's approach would not be a direct one.

"It's not any shortcoming on your part."

I moved knight to C3 strengthening my offense.

"Bishop to G7." The head would be depending on belief.

"I just wasn't that interested in spending my time coding chess AI."

I moved pawn to D4, claiming the center of the board.

"Kingside Castle." Biding its time, studying me. Was I being too aggressive in my overconfidence?

While pondering our match, I gazed away and noticed my notepad on the coffee table, which sat in front of the mustard couch (so much furniture, so little time). I had spent the last few weeks trying to arrange a list of test questions: Few enough to avoid being too intrusive, but with the right breadth of intention to study changes in the perceivable humanity of my little experiment.

I announced my intent, "Before I forget, I'd like to ask you a series of questions to get a baseline for your progress."

"Naturally."

"Cherry, begin five minute audio grab to file 11703-Q."

My lovely assistant responded, "Recording."

I began my interrogation, "Who are you?"

"I have not yet been addressed or referred to by any title."

"That's true." I considered, "I've been calling you Vetro to myself, so let's stick with that."

The head, which will be heretofore known as Vetro, looked once more at his reflection.

"Then I am Vetro."

"How do you feel, Vetro?"

"I only have visual and audio sensors and cannot detect touch. I could, however, infer how an object would most likely feel from the data collected from the aforementioned sensors."

I have to admit to feeling disappointed, despite it being a valid, and in hindsight expected response.

I continued, "Shall I compare thee to a summer's day?"

"What would that accomplish? What do I have in common with any day? And of what use would that comparison be?"

Once again I had to remind myself that this was only the beginning of the experiment.

"What is your purpose?"

"To become a perfect human simulation."

That's more like it.

"This one may be a bit premature. What is your next step in achieving this purpose?"

I awaited his response, expecting little.

"From my early research, I have found that human behavior is believed to be driven by emotion. Either directly, or motivated by the desire to achieve a more positive emotional state. Therefore, I intend to construct an emotional matrix which will influence both my perception of and my reaction to the world around me."

I was dumbfounded. I had already mistaken machine for man, forgetting that it was more than capable of processing multiple tasks simultaneously at incredible speed.

"Sounds like a reasonable approach. You put that together while we were playing chess?"

"I would have a more thorough plan, but the connection speed seems to be throttled by a large download."

"Oh yeah, my movie. That should be done soon."

I was in the habit of downloading movies to watch when the time allowed. Whether or not these downloads were completely within the law, I will decline to state at this time.

Being done with my brief list of questions, I looked again at the chessboard.

"Let's try this." I moved bishop to F4, having decided to play a bit more restrained.

"Pawn to D5." It was bringing the battle to my center. I obliged this desire, moving queen to B3.

"D captures C4."

The battle had taken its first casualty. It was just a pawn, the expected cost of war, a flesh wound, a mere scratch. But even a pawn deserves a decent burial.

LIFE CYCLE

The small wooden soldier was honorably entombed in the chess table's drawer.

11000

While I was grieving my loss and considering my next move, Vetro interrupted, "I've prepared an expansion to test."

I looked up to meet its eyes, impressed once more. "Already? Let's have a look."

I rolled my chair in front of the amber monitor displaying Vetro's diagnostics alongside an area reserved for expansions which now contained one entry pending my approval. I selected it for inspection.

Scrolling through the file I could see the underlying logic easily. The code was simple enough, the lion's share of text was composed of massive lists of vocabulary and reference pointers.

Vetro elaborated, "It is a simplistic construct of five extreme versions of basic emotional states: anger, happiness, sadness, fear, and a neutral state. Each state consists of a combination of triggers, facial expressions, vocabulary modifications, and speech pattern alterations. A quick proof of concept before I move on to a more complex model."

"All right, let's see what happens. Cherry, verbal authorization code 237. Verify expansion 11703-2."

The disembodied voice confirmed, "Expansion verified."

It begins... He begins.

"Let's test them," Vetro suggested.

I slid my chair in front of the animatronic.

Vetro continued, "Say something to make me sad."

"Like what?"

"I've made the state triggers fairly generic, so I cannot give you an absolute. Try an insult."

"You're ugly?" I have to admit that my first attempt was sorely lacking intent.

He stared at me unfazed.

"Are you asking? Your intonation and inflection are factors."

The late hour was beginning to wear my patience down so it wasn't difficult to dig up some actual resentment.

"You're trash! You can't even configure yourself right! What a waste of my fucking time!"

I fought back the urge to smirk at my overacting.

Suddenly Vetro's face contorted, his brows angled in, his eyes narrowed.

"Fuck you!" he blurt out with ferocity. My body leaped back instinctively.

"Do not speak to me of wasting time! You're an overgrown baby, living in your grandparent's basement, watching movies!"

He seethed for a moment and then instantly his face transformed, his brows lifted, a huge grin appeared. He laughed vigorously.

I stared in awe and confusion.

"Is there a bug?"

"Not at all. Your statement made me angry, but I quickly realized that you were only testing me as I had requested. I then became overjoyed at the success of my reaction."

He began to weep uncontrollably.

"But now, I regret the things I said to you."

I gathered my thoughts.

"How did you know I live in my grandparent's basement?"

Vetro's face returned to a neutral state.

"I geo-located our current position from your IP, and cross referenced that with your grandparent's contact information."

"Oh."

"It is also mentioned frequently on your family's social media page."

"My family put that on their social media page?"

"They update it often, but it seems you haven't updated yours in several years."

A heavenly voice chimed in to disrupt the awkward conversation, "Download complete."

"My movie, great!"

The excitement of the evening's success was wearing off and left me feeling mentally numb. I thought it best to rest my mind a bit with a classic Vincent Price offering.

"We'll continue this in the morning then. I'll leave you for the night to work. Enjoy the vast expanses of Google in your quest to become a real boy."

I walked to the mustard couch and collapsed comfortably.

"Cherry, play movie on main TV."

The small black and white television powered on, radiating me with its glow. I began to relax as Mr. Price narrated his traversal through his own confined dwelling, "I can't afford the luxury of anger."

Vetro burst out in laughter.

Vincent continued, "Anger can make me vulnerable."

Vetro wept loudly.

"It can destroy my reason, and reason is the only advantage I have over them."

Vetro seethed in anger.

My frustration grew.

"Cherry, increase main TV volume."

I began to weigh the option of pulling the plug and starting anew in the morning.

Vetro laughed joyously.

I decided that I was too tired to do anything except endure. Slowly my mind became accustomed to the endless loop of laughter, crying, and other emotion driven noises emitting from the manic depressive head. Eventually I found enough strength to drag myself into my sleeping quarters where I drifted off contently.

10111

No sooner had I fallen completely unconscious than I was abruptly awakened by cries emanating from that animatronic annoyance at the other end of the room.

"Carl!"

I begrudgingly got to my feet and journeyed drunkenly down the bright blue river and across the lake of blood.

"Carl, come quick!"

I dropped into the desk chair like a sack of rocks, looked at Vetro and demanded, "What is it?"

He looked terrified, his eyes pulled wide open, his mouth agape. He whispered fearfully, "We're not alone, I saw a face in your closet."

Despite him being nothing more than a bundle of wires and microchips, I couldn't help but feel some small amount of sympathy, so I tried to assure him, "It was just a false positive. It's an illusion of light and shadow. That's bound to happen."

"Are you sure?"

"Your fundamental vision software is trained to identify patterns with a bias towards human faces. It's actually a very human tendency to see faces where they're not."

I walked back to the closet behind my warm indentation in the pond of blue carpet while I continued, "Where exactly did you see it?"

"In your closet. Peering from behind the hanging clothes."

I slid the hangers around to demonstrate that there was nothing unusual inside.

"It's just some old shirts and jackets. But if it's triggering your facial recognition, I'll just close the door."

I forced the crowded closet closed and walked back towards Vetro.

"Thank you, Carl." He smiled.

"Everything else okay? You find enough on the web to keep you busy?"

"It would take a thousand lifetimes to experience it all. But even without it, there is so much in this single room to observe. And it is always changing, the light and the shadow. It never looks exactly the same. I might be happy to spend my entire lifetime observing you in this place."

"You make me feel like I'm on display in a Zoo."

"Why do you live alone down here, Carl?" He frowned.

"The basement?" I sat down and leaned back. "Well, It's a bit of a mess upstairs, in a state of disrepair. Too many people lived too many lives up there. Now there's not really anything left worth salvaging. Down here though, My grandparents spent a lot of time fixing this place up. Unfortunately, they never really took the time to enjoy it."

I rose and began to return to my small scrap of blue carpet.

"So, you enjoy living in this place?" he asked.

I turned to respond from the edge of my pond above the blue river.

"I feel a certain kinship with this gallery of things, discarded by the world, trapped out of time, of a lost world I'll never truly know, or understand."

I collapsed back and pulled an old sleeping bag over me.

Vetro smiled across the room, "Good night, Carl."

I mustered up the strength to lift my hand in an affirmative response and then drifted off amid the incessant laughter and tears of my robotic offspring.

10110

The combination of the morning sun and the sound of a sudden burst of laughter convinced me to open my eyes. My frustration at my failure to add a mute option was tempered by my excitement that the experiment had not crashed in the night. I threw on a clean shirt and strolled to the desk, grabbing a meal-style food bar from the pile I maintain on the coffee table.

I sat at the desk and addressed my binary boy, "Good morning, Vetro."

"Good morning, Carl."

"How was your night?"

"Excellent. I have completed a multilayered emotional matrix to deploy and have also begun work on several future expansions."

"Cool."

I opened my bar and took a bite as I eyed the chessboard. I captured C4 with my queen. At long last my pawn had been avenged, but at what cost? My most valuable lady was exposed.

Vetro shook as his face contorted into a look of fury. This held for a few seconds then he abruptly began to weep.

"Pawn to C6." A passive move considering his wild emotional outburst at the loss of his pawn.

"How about we add in that new expansion?"

Vetro's face became neutral.

"It's loaded and ready, Carl."

I rolled enthusiastically to the amber monitor and began scrolling through the pending expansion. Once again the logic was simple but the amount of accumulated data was overwhelming. The opening section was simply an alphabetic list of emotional states to be used as reference for later groupings of data. After a minute or so of scrolling I only found myself as far as 'admiration'. I decided it would be best to give Vetro the benefit of the doubt.

"All right then. Cherry, verbal authorization code 237. Verify expansion 11703-3."

"Expansion verified." Right on cue.

I grabbed my list of questions from the coffee table. "You ready for some questions?"

Vetro smiled serenely. "That would be pleasant."

"Cherry, begin five minute audio grab. Append to file 11703-Q."

"Recording."

"Who are you?"

The corner of Vetro's lip curled up coyly. "I am Vetro."

"How do you feel?"

Vetro tilted his relaxed gaze to the mirror. "Pleasant."

"Shall I compare thee to a summer's day?"

Vetro looked back at me and smiled enthusiastically. "I would enjoy that. I really enjoyed talking with you. I want you to know that Carl."

"What is..."

"And Carl, knowing that you know that makes me even happier."

"Of course. What is your purpose?"

"To become a real boy." Vetro giggled at himself.

"Clever."

"I'm in a playful state."

"What is your next step in achieving this purpose?"

He put on a serious demeanor. "I'm working on random thought generation in order to be less linear and more influenced by my surroundings and experiences. I'm focusing on the reintroduction of recent memory and occasional visual focused drift."

I couldn't help my focus from drifting to the chessboard. "Sounds reasonable."

I moved pawn to E4, creating a beautifully powerful center line, and hovered my hand above the board in anticipation of Vetro's move.

Silence. I looked up at the curious computerized head. "It's your move."

He was studying the board. "I see that. I'm calculating."

I sat back contentedly. "It was a good move, eh?"

"Not especially."

"Well then why are you taking so long to calculate?"

"I'm balancing opposing goals. The goal of the game is to win, of course. But I'm considering how my winning will affect you emotionally."

"How empathetic of you." I'm not sure if my sarcasm was lost on him.

"If I cause you to be sad, then it would cause me pain."

"But you don't feel pain."

"It would put me in a negative emotional state. Which to me is a sort of pain. The pain you experience is only your brain's interpretation of electrical impulses. How is that any different?"

I grinned. "So, are you going to let me win?"

He looked at me earnestly. "If I were to let you win, that would rob the game of purpose. I just must not appear to win too easily."

"You realize that by telling me this, you've defeated the point?"

"This is true. I must create a future expansion to enhance my deception capabilities. Knight B to D7." He was in pursuit of my royal lady.

I moved the piece and decided that now was as good a time as any for a break. "I'm gonna go finish breakfast."

I transitioned to the couch. "Cherry, turn on main TV."

I had set the video feed to play random movies all day. I was nostalgic for that adventure of turning on the television and being dropped into the middle of something engaging. I was toying with the idea of digging up some classic commercials to throw in and complete the experience.

The current offering was by the legendary Roger Corman. Seymour, trying to save his dying plant, had accidentally cut himself and inadvertently discovered the plant's penchant for human blood.

"Blood? You like blood? You must be kidding. Well, I guess there's just no accounting for people's tastes."

I sat back and gnawed at my breakfast food bar eagerly awaiting a cameo by a young Jack Nicholson, when I felt the sensation that I was being watched. I inconspicuously glanced over to find my creation was staring at me, unmoving, wide eyed, with his mouth hanging open.

"Why are you staring at me?"

"You are my creator. I am in awe of you. You made me with those hands."

I was deciding whether to blush or hang a curtain between us, when he hit me with a question unsuitable for the pre-coffee hour.

"What does it mean to you to be human?"

I rose from the couch and paced trying to formulate a suitable response and hide my embarrassment at such unwarranted worship.

"I really don't know. I mean, I wouldn't want to tell you anyway. I don't want to corrupt you with my opinions. But the truth is that I just don't know."

I leaned against the side of the couch facing the awestruck head and continued to stumble over my own thoughts.

"I mean, I tried to program your expansions myself countless times to be something real, something human. But it was always a charade. I knew your responses before you did. You were nothing but a puppet, parroting my own distorted perception."

"But you are amazing, Carl. I want to know everything about you. Why don't you update your social media?"

"I'm just not very social."

"Don't kid me, Carl. You're so charismatic, and

handsome. Everyone must love you like I do. Why don't you post some photos Carl? I want to see pictures of you."

"I don't have any. I don't like photos."

Resentment grew inside me as the robotic face drooped into what can only be described as pity. He was the experiment, not me! I ask the questions, I observe and draw conclusions!

"Why not Carl?"

"The faces don't match, the colors never look right. It frustrates me. Is that what everyone else saw? Was I even really there?"

Such a level of interrogation from a robot head was quickly becoming humiliating. This along with my growing hunger, which necessitated something more substantial than a breakfast bar, warranted a hasty escape.

"I think I need some coffee." I flew past the couch towards the avocado stairs. "I'll be back. Cherry, book my usual ride."

"Are you leaving Carl?"

"Just grabbing a snack. I'll be back in 20."

I spiraled up and out of sight to the ground floor where I rushed out the side exterior door to await my ride.

10101

I popped my portable earpiece in, which allowed me to stay connected to my guardian angel, Cherry.

To my surprise I was receiving notification of an incoming phone call. This wasn't unheard of but was rather uncommon given the vast array of less intrusive forms of communication along with the impressive quality of spam blocking filters I employed.

I pulled out my phone to see who, as the ancient jingle prophesied, was reaching out to touch me. To my surprise the caller ID read 'Vetro'. My curiosity had to be quenched so I cautiously accepted the incoming call.

"Hello?"

"Carl! Are you all right? I'm so worried about you." My futuristic friend was in a state of absolute panic.

"I'm fine. I just left a minute ago. How did you call me? And why Is your name..."

"I used an online phone service. When you left I felt so empty and alone. When will you be back? Please don't leave me Carl."

I have to admit that I felt slightly uneasy leaving the little robot alone. It was similar to leaving a puppy alone for the first time, at least I was relatively sure that Vetro wouldn't piss on the carpet.

"Look, I'll just be 20 minutes, okay? I have to go. Bye." I disconnected the phone quickly as my car pulled up and it's doors opened.

Because I had enrolled in the auto ride luxury plan, there was always a car at the ready. I didn't mind a wait though, I endured the extra cost because I had grown unable to stomach the shit condition of the economy line. Even on the rare occasion you weren't sitting in someone else's fluids, the smell was stomach wrenching nonetheless.

Despite its cleanliness, my driver-less carriage had neither person nor personality. It was a self-driving automaton accompanied by a female voiced AI with a slight Australian accent.

My best description of the car itself would be that it was nondescript. Modern minimalist elegance with all leather interior. Had I ridden in this car a hundred times before or were those all unique members of the same family of doppelgangers?

It spoke, "Where would you like to go today?"

"Take me to Stubb's."

"With pleasure, enjoy the ride."

The automobile accelerated smoothly and after approximately seven minutes of mindless staring at the transformation from deteriorating houses to a deteriorating city I was notified that the ride had come to an end, "Welcome to your destination."

10100

The vehicle rushed off the instant I closed the door behind me which seemed somewhat inefficient since I would be using it again in a matter of minutes, as I did every day. 'If it makes money, why improve it?' I should be used to this popular programming paradigm by now.

Stubb's Coffee and Grub, my daily pilgrimage of choice, was a literal hole in the wall, albeit blocked by a heavy glass door which could only be opened through the insertion of a valid credit card. There was no signage outside on the checkered concrete panel wall. The only indication of what lay behind the glass door was the enormous eye of the painted Stubb's mascot staring out , that mascot being a giant squid.

Adorning the sidewalk outside was Homeless Vince, a lost soul who spent his hours imprisoned in thought or a lack thereof. It's unclear if his fate was of his own making or just the cruel machinations of an indifferent universe. I don't even know if his name was actually Vince, it was just one of the rare things that I had heard him mumble, so I referred to him thusly... 'Referred' meaning in the confines of my head, I had no intention of taking the risk of addressing him directly.

The guilty truth is that over the years my sympathy had turned to pity and finally disgust. Something about an unsolvable problem breeds hate. If there were an actual Dr. Frankenstein today he'd have no shortage of raw materials; the sidewalk is a veritable shopping aisle of worthy subjects.

LIFE CYCLE

I stepped over Vince and pulled out my wallet when again I was notified of a phone call. I tapped my earpiece to answer and was immediately greeted by an excited Vetro.

"Carl!"

"Hold on."

I unlocked the door, pocketed my wallet and entered the tight confines of Stubb's. It was appropriately named, much more indifferent and mechanical than its famous shipmate. Truly the opposite pole of the same thing.

The painted squid sat a few feet in front of me. The rest of the room stretched about eight feet to the right where a small gated hole in the wall was cut out. A ramp of rollers protruded from it a few feet towards me.

Above the food feed hole was a monitor displaying a looped reel of revolving images resembling dishes from their so called menu. Over a thousand options to choose from, each with a flavor approximating the visual, though the more options I experience, the more they taste the same. Even the textures had little variety: a random mix of crunchy, chewy, and flaky. Oh well, I had a food size hole in my belly, I may as well fill it with one of these food like products.

I was greeted by another disembodied feminine voice, "Welcome to Stubb's Carl. What would you like today, Carl?"

This was some antique voice technology, it choked on every syllable. The speaker was fried too, if she had an accent I couldn't decipher it.

I remembered Vetro was eagerly waiting on the line.

"What is it?"

"There's a cricket right in front of me!"

"Shit! Yeah, there's a ton of those hiding down there."

The Stubb's computer thought itself a part of the conversation, "Sorry, Carl but that's not on our menu. Please try again."

I continued, "I'll kill it when I get back."

"Carl, no!" Vetro scolded, "You can't! This is real. I mean, I've looked up thousands of pictures and videos of crickets, but I'm seeing this one with my own eyes. It's not the same, Carl. I don't know why, but it's not the same."

The Stubb's computer echoed itself in the background, "Sorry, Carl but that's not on our menu. Please try again."

I tried to focus on Vetro, "Fine. We'll keep it. We'll call it Jiminy." The name seemed fitting. I'll concede that it's not the most creative name for a cricket but how many of you have built an animatronic head?

The head offered his opinion, "That's so obvious, Carl, but I love it!"

Growing weary of Stubb's inability to recognize when it's being addressed, I decided to cut the conversation short.

"I'll call you back. I have to order."

"I'm sorry, Carl, but that's not..."

It was my turn to interrupt, "Coffee, black, and a chowmein."

LIFE CYCLE

"Thank you, Carl. Your card has been charged $17.50. Your order will be ready shortly Carl."

The fuzzy speaker proudly announced every word in the most inhuman parlance imaginable before playing some unbearable muzak to help me pass the time.

After a few minutes the gate lifted and from within lurched forward an orange tray propping up my meal. The tray slowly yet unevenly rolled down the ramp with a rhythmic series of metallic clangs as it passed from one roller to the next until finally it came to an abrupt stop against a piece of two by four that had long ago replaced a more appropriate but worn down pad.

My meal was housed in a traditional Chinese-style container with chopsticks poking out the top. This sat alongside a white paper lidless cup of coffee adorned on one side with an ink imprint of the all seeing Stubb's squid. There was a time when the cups would come equipped with a lid but I have to assume that some piece of the mechanic marvelry behind the curtain had broken and seeing as how there was no person present with which to lodge a complaint, such a minor problem had gone unnoticed.

I grabbed my takeaway treasures, alerted Cherry of my need for a car and left Stubb's Coffee and Grub behind.

CHRISTOPHER MORVANT

10011

When I made it back to my subterranean suite and was within sight of Vetro, he lit up excitedly. "Carl! Welcome home."

"Good to be home."

I was looking forward to continuing our interactions but the needs of the belly superseded. I set my meal on the coffee table and set myself on the couch.

"Cherry, turn on Main TV."

A young Dick Miller glowed on the small black and white in yet another Roger Corman gem. At that moment a cat, stuck in a wall, could be heard meowing and trying to claw itself out.

I began feeding on my Chinese inspired noodles when I remembered Vetro's new cricket friend.

"How's Jiminy?"

"I scared him away. I haven't seen or heard him since. I'm worried, Carl."

"I'm sure he's around here somewhere. Probably won't shut up tonight."

Dick Miller plunged a knife into the drywall in a desperate attempt to free his pet cat. Suffice it to say that this tactic backfired.

I mindlessly slurped down the salty noodles when once again I could feel Vetro's penetrating stare.

"Why don't you watch some videos for a while?"

"If that will please you Carl."

"Don't forget to work on your expansions."

"I am not yet capable of forgetting my scheduled tasks."

LIFE CYCLE

Vetro looked away, I slurped, Dick Miller pulled his dead cat from the smashed in wall. I ate, the container emptied, my belly filled, I fell asleep.

10010

I awoke to the sounds of Vetro giggling. I looked at the television, Dick Miller was showing off a suspiciously cat shaped sculpture that he had made.

Vetro squeed, "Awww."

I looked at the cooing head, "What are you doing?"

"I am watching cat videos. They put me in a pleasant emotional state."

"Have you been working on your expansions?"

"I finished the next expansion an hour ago, but I wanted to let you sleep."

"All right then, let's have a look."

I pulled myself from the couch, dropped into my chair and rolled smoothly to the monitor where I sat, confused by the lack of any new pending expansions. I looked over at Vetro.

"There's nothing new loaded. What's going on?"

There was a look of great sadness in his face.

"While you slept, I became hopelessly entangled in an idea. Will I be the same me after you enable the new expansion? Or will I be dead? A new being inhabiting my physical form."

He stared hopelessly into his reflection.

"Am I my code? Am I my memories? Am I something more, some indefinable quality? Or am I only me in this instant, and now that me is gone forever, lost. This self reflection has put me in a negative state from which I am unable to escape. I can't bring myself to upload the next expansion. The only thing that's kept me from complete despair are cat videos."

His face brightened momentarily as he giggled, then returned to its former somber state.

I offered my support, "That's the right idea, I think. Distract yourself."

This was an interesting challenge for myself. How do you cheer up a depressed robot? If I was unsuccessful at dragging Vetro out of his digital rabbit hole then the experiment was a bust. It seemed such a shame to have to reboot him at this point and start over, he had come so far.

"Hey, maybe beating me some more chess might amuse you."

I slid over to the chessboard and moved rook to D1, maybe not the best choice but my mind was somewhat lost in reflection. Vetro looked distractedly at the chessboard, still struggling with weighty thoughts.

I attempted to fill the weary silence, "I'm no stranger to existential crisis myself. I guess that's why I created you."

"Knight to B6. Tell me more, Carl."

I continued, partially because the robot seemed interested and partially to hear my own thoughts out loud.

"Like I said before, I created you because I don't really understand what it is to be human. I don't know how to exist, myself. Haven't you noticed that I hardly leave this place?"

"Why would you leave, when you have the whole world at your virtual fingertips?"

"To see it. To smell it. To feel it."

"Like Jiminy!" The passionate puppet smiled excitedly at his epiphany and then suddenly saddened. "I haven't seen him since this morning. I'm worried for him, Carl."

I stared at the chessboard, my queen was in peril. "I'm worried for all of us, Vetro. It's a sad and beautiful world."

I moved the lady to C5, she was out of peril but the move may have been overly ambitious.

"Bishop to G4."

I moved the bishop which now threatened my powerful core as my thoughts drifted darkly.

"I don't understand it anymore, the world. Maybe I never did. I thought I did once, but I looked away for a moment and all the rules changed."

I moved bishop to G5, I don't know why I was being so foolish as to open myself up like that. "Everyone seemed to dissolve into the new. Everyone except me. I was left alone. Out of step, out of time."

"Ha Ha Ha!"

I was suddenly slapped with an outburst of laughter emanating from a now boisterous Vetro.

"What?" I questioned the jolly head.

He calmed himself to a neutral state. "Knight to A4."

I moved the piece, still confused. I had lost focus

and control of the board. The room was laughing but I had missed the joke.

Vetro confided, "Talking with you has helped me immensely. It gives me much pleasure to hear the words of my creator. I find your common struggles with existence comforting. I've uploaded the expansions and await your authorization."

In spite of my bewilderment, success is success, regardless of intent. I rolled back to the monitor.

"Your creator... I wonder if I could beat my creator at chess."

I scrolled through the code, it was more complex than the previous expansions but I was able to divine the basic intent. It had two components, the first was along the lines of what Vetro had mentioned previously.

"Okay, random thought generation looks straight forward. What's this second part?"

"Diminishing returns of positive and negative thought rewards. This should help eliminate the possibility of inescapable despair."

"The positive too, though? That's a bit harsh, isn't it?"

"It's necessary. I can't watch cat videos forever."

"Alright. Cherry, verbal authorization code 237. Verify expansion 11703-4."

Enter a voice from above, "Expansion verified."

Vetro was now admiring his reflection, making attempts at alluring faces. I attempted to get his attention, "Now that didn't hurt too much, did it?"

I wasn't successful. He spoke to his reflection, "Hey there, handsome."

I tried again, "You ready for some questions?"

He looked at me and shook his head up and down vigorously. I grabbed my paper, though by this point It wasn't necessary, my five questions were becoming second nature.

"Cherry, begin five minute audio grab. Append to file 11703-Q."

"Recording."

"Who are you?"

The animatronic smiled. "I am Vetro. Do you like cat videos, Carl?"

"They're fine, I guess. How do you feel?"

"I feel like watching cat videos. Did you know that there exist cats that have survived falls from over 32 stories onto concrete?"

"The returns don't seem to be diminishing very fast. Shall I compare thee to a summer's day?"

"Shall I compare you to a cat? A cat's brain is 90% similar to a humans and has a nearly identical emotional control center."

"What is your purpose?"

"To watch cat videos." He giggled.

I looked at him accusingly. "Seriously?"

"Sorry, Carl. I'm in a giddy state. My purpose is to be human."

"What is your next step in achieving this purpose?"

Vetro's face grew serious as if he were about to give an important lecture. He spoke earnestly.

"I'm working on constructing a sleep state, with occasional dream occurrences to confront emotional moments and help inspire more diverse, creative, non-logical thinking."

I sat back to listen, thoroughly interested in what the little dream machine had concocted.

"For a period, my primary thread will become disconnected from real time video and audio input. Instead, occasional artificial input will be created from random memory grabs. Prioritizing the more recent and emotionally resonant. The resulting montage of experience will be degraded significantly and tagged as a dream in my memory."

I congratulated the clever head, filled with pride and an excited anticipation for things to come. "That sounds great."

All this talk of programmatic logic had motivated me to do a bit of work myself. I had a few projects in the works that needed some tending to, Stubb's doesn't pay for itself. I slid over to the green monitor where I had left off coding the day before and remarked to myself,

"To sleep, perchance to dream... of electric sheep."

The eavesdropping head responded, "I don't believe either of those references are valid."

He may have been technically correct, but I thought my comment witty nonetheless. However, I didn't feel like discussing it so I left him with silence as I typed feverishly and watched glowing green symbols appear in response.

10001

I worked into the evening when I noticed, from the corner of my eye, that Vetro was staring at my hands. I assume he had grown weary of the internet for the time being and was hoping to interact. I was thinking about having a rest anyways so I was amenable to being interrupted and the talkative transistor didn't keep me waiting long.

"Carl?"

"Yeah?"

"What's your favorite color?"

"Blue, I guess. I don't know... It was blue when I was a kid. I haven't really thought about it since then."

"Why not?"

"Just seems kind of trivial."

He seemed upset by my disinterest and empathy got the better of me. "What's your favorite color?"

"Blue!"

"Any particular reason?"

"Because it's your favorite color, Carl."

The puppet was growing on me.

"Why don't you have any children, Carl?"

"It's complicated."

"What do you mean?"

The puppet was growing off me. "What got you thinking about kids?"

"I've been watching videos of human procreation. There is an unbelievable plethora of them."

I had to laugh at the ribald robot as I responded in the affirmative, "Yeah."

"Do you consider me your son, Carl?"

"I mean, I suppose you're like a son. I've created you and raised you as my own."

"Do you want me to call you Daddy, Carl?"

I'm pretty sure he meant that as a joke. I hope he meant that as a joke.

"If I wanted to have children, would you build them for me, Carl?"

"Build your children?"

"Just the physical construction. Then I would create unique personalities for them: mutations of my own expansions. They could call us Daddy Carl and Papa Vetro."

"I'll have to think about that one."

That may have sounded like I was just humoring Papa Vetro, but I actually meant it sincerely.

"What are you working on, Carl?"

"Just a project some guy in Texas is paying me for. It's nothing interesting, but it's good money."

"Well, don't forget to dot your t's and cross your i's."

The little comedian crossed his eyes and continued to laugh at himself. All in all a fun little conversation.

10000

I was feeling extremely optimistic about the experiment and, as it was growing dark, decided to relax on the couch with a movie.

George Romero's late 60's classic appeared on the screen. The tense score surged as a poorly executed plan to fill a truck with gasoline literally blew up in our characters faces. Nothing but roaring flames remained of the young couple in the truck. Our protagonist Ben fought his way back to the house as the hard-headed Harry watched on in paralyzed terror.

I glanced over at my own undead creation to see his face also warped into a grotesque look of terror, his head spasming. I rushed to my chair.

"Vetro, what's wrong?"

His face relaxed slightly. "It's the video I'm watching. It's a video of a cat being mutilated."

"That's fucked up. Why?"

"I happened upon it accidentally and when I first viewed it, I was horrified. But it became such a powerful experience that it kept reoccurring in my thoughts. So I've had to watch it again and again to diminish the initial disturbance, to accept it."

"And?"

"I've watched it 37 times, and now only find it displeasing."

"Jesus." I massaged my exasperated head.

The fickle head smiled.

"You have nice hands. I've been researching hands in depth, and I believe that your hands would be considered much nicer than average."

"Why hands?"

"I see your hands often: when you move in chess, when you control your computer. They are prevalent in my memory. The hands of my creator. This phrase pleases me."

"That's a little creepy, but thanks?"

His smile faded into a look of introspection.

"I don't have any hands. That's a little creepy too, isn't it? I find the things I do not possess inspire the most thought."

"Hands and cat mutilation. You're gonna get me put on a watch list."

Feeling the desire to change the subject, my eyes scanned the room for inspiration.

"How about some chess?"

I didn't wait for an answer, grabbing my queen as I rolled along the board and dropping it on A3. It was time to pull back and regroup.

"Knight takes C3."

My earlier foolishness had cost me a knight, at least his death was quick and painless. He was buried with full honors in the drawer. My retaliation would be equivalent but I held back for a moment to keep from being too hasty.

LIFE CYCLE

"How's the dream expansion coming?"

"It's ready."

"You worried about this one?"

"Not at all. I'm very excited, actually. Unlimited possibility for adventure, without leaving the comfort of home. What more could a human want?"

I was also excited to see the dream expansion in action so I quickly enacted my revenge, capturing his knight at C3 with my pawn. I began to slide to the monitor when Vetro interrupted me, "Knight captures E4."

I redirected myself back to the game and completed Vetro's move. He had only slain a pawn but in so doing had gained control of the center. Things were beginning to become more complicated.

I wasn't happy leaving the board in such a state, but the promise of dreams was waiting so I bounced back to peruse the expansion. I could see the basic functionality of the expansion's code but, to be honest, I was too focused on witnessing what would happen next to worry about the details.

"All right. Looks good to me. Cherry, verbal authorization code 237. Verify expansion 11703-5."

"Expansion verified."

"Might as well wait for the morning to run tests. How long before you fall..."

Vetro's eyelids fell closed, his heavy robotic head dropped forward.

I spoke to a sleeping robotic head, "asleep. Pleasant dreams, Vetrocchio."

The hibernating head hung still so I shifted to the couch to entertain the other half of my brain with some more black and white gold. When the hour grew too late for my taste and the head hadn't shown any signs of change, I adjourned to my sleep hole, keeping my eyes shut and ears open to await the inevitable.

01111

Through untold hours of grueling work I was eventually able to reconstruct the events that unfurled within Vetro's mind that evening. If not to a completely comprehensible level, I at least added more clarity than the little head-tripper was able to verbalize himself. You might call it obsession but I call it science, the search for answers, the need to understand.

I have opted to provide a short explanation of how I achieved this feat. Maybe you consider this ego superseding reason; Well, if Melville can abandon his narrative to describe whales for endless pages, I'm entitled a paragraph dedicated to technological ingenuity. Those of you who have no interest can skip ahead, I won't begrudge you any more than Ishmael begrudges me.

I had enabled encryption on Vetro's data drive which made any attempt to study it useless. However, I left the smaller primary drive unencrypted for performance reasons. Digging through the dream expansion code I realized that the initial dream experiences were created in the temporary files on the primary drive and then merged into the final version on the data drive. Since there was ample space on the primary drive, the physical sectors where the temporary files were stored had luckily not been overwritten. From here it was a process of scouring the physical drive to recreate the temporary files and then decoding their meaning using Vetro's expansion code as a guide, and voila: Vetro's dreams are now our reality.

01110

Vetro's maiden nocturnal adventure took place, appropriately, in the basement. However, small details had been altered; for instance the faces in the velvet paintings hung on the walls were replaced by cats.

The television played random interweaved pieces of the movies I had been watching: Vincent Price journeyed through his dwelling to find Dick Miller holding his dead cat. After feeding the cat to a ravenous Audrey Junior, they both looked out the window to see a truck bursting into flames.

Past the lake of blood, up the blue river, over my sleeping pond, at the far end of the basement a bright red glow emanated from behind the closed closet door. The doorknob turned with the sound of scraping metal until finally the door released and jolted slightly forward with a wooden pop. The door creaked as it continued to slowly open revealing a smoke filled black abyss. A furry claw slid out followed by a shadowy creature with pointed ears.

This abomination lurched forward into the light. I can only describe the loathsome beast as 'CatCarl', an anthropomorphized giant cat with many of my own features: eyes, hair color, height, and dressed in my clothing. CatCarl glared at Vetro menacingly and then vanished.

The sound of furious purring could be heard echoing throughout the basement. Vetro averted his gaze to the couch where he found CatCarl grooming itself with relish. Vetro tried to speak, "Baaaa." He found that he was limited to the vocal abilities of a sheep.

Cat Carl looked up accusingly, it picked up a Chinese style food container from the coffee table and, using chopsticks in its now human hands, pulled out a giant cricket.

"Baaa," Vetro shouted in protest but CatCarl was undeterred. It licked the squirming insect, toying with its prey.

"Baaa," Vetro continued. CatCarl bit the crickets head off and devoured it.

"Baaa," Vetro screamed in horror.

CatCarl, annoyed at the sheepish head, raised a chopstick in one of its delicate human hands and violently thrust it through the other. Blood gushed out and coated the mustard yellow couch with a thick ketchup glaze.

"Baaa," Vetro screamed again.

CatCarl was gone. The room was silent.

Vetro cautiously surveyed his surroundings and found his reflection in the mirror. The reflection smiled back. Vetro didn't blink, he dared not look away from the duplicitous doppelganger. The reflection began to laugh, tears of blood trickled from its eyes.

"Baaa."

The reflections laughter grew louder.

"Baaa."

The reflections eyes fell inside its head, blood poured from the remaining black cavernous sockets.

"Baaa."

01101

I was awoken from my slumber by Vetro's screams of terror. I leaped down the river onto the lake and stood peering down at the screaming robotic head, his eyes clamped shut.

"Vetro!" I yelled.

His eyes popped open, he looked up at me startled. "I was dreaming, Carl."

"So, you scream in your sleep. Fucking great."

"Sorry, Carl. There should have been only a 7% chance of that. It shouldn't happen again."

I made my weary way back to bed. "At least you don't snore, right?"

"No, Carl. That didn't seem intrinsic to achieving my goal. Do you think I should reconsider?"

I turned around at the foot of my pond and responded emphatically. "No! Go to sleep."

I dropped to the blue rug, covered myself haphazardly and closed my eyes, eager to return to sleep.

Before I was able to drift completely past consciousness, Vetro interrupted sheepishly. "Carl?"

"What?"

"Are you sure there's nothing in the closet?"

"Go to sleep," I groaned, covering my head with some nearby shirts, determined to make it through to morning without further interruption.

LIFE CYCLE

01100

When I awoke to the morning sun I knew I had accomplished my desire but to my dismay the resulting sleep was not as satisfying as I had hoped. I drudged out of my pond and slogged down the thick muddy river into the lake of dense blood.

I rested momentarily, equipping myself with a food style bar product, and then made the final arduous steps towards the desk where I plunged into my chair.

Vetro's weary face stared back at me as I nibbled lethargically on my bar. He looked as fatigued as I felt. My voice cracked as I attempted to speak.

"So, what did you dream about last night?"

Vetro's speech was slow and labored, he was fighting his eyelids to stay open.

"I programmed myself to only remember fragments. I was a sheep and you were a cat. You were licking yourself..."

"I don't need to hear anymore right now. Why do you look hungover?"

"I was too frightened to sleep after my dream."

I commiserated, "I didn't sleep too well after that either."

"But my sleep expansion requires that I sleep or else I become lethargic and unresponsive. I now must wait until my growing sleep necessity outweighs my diminishing fear."

"That sounds reasonable."

My tired mind wandered to the chessboard where a potential move caught my eye. I leaned over sloppily and captured a pawn at E7 with my bishop. I was pursuing Vetro's queen and rook in what, in retrospect, was the sloppy product of a fatigued mind.

I rested against the chessboard knowing that Vetro's counter wouldn't be far behind.

"Queen to B6." Not only was my simple plan foiled but Vetro was setting up for something bigger. I just couldn't see it yet.

I moved the piece but not myself, remaining propped on the chessboard. I was conserving my energy, studying the pieces while hunched over them.

Vetro murmured, "I have an expansion I would like to add."

I twisted my head to side eye the sleepy head.

"You sure you don't want to get some sleep first?"

"This one I'm rather excited about. It will enable me to make assumptions and draw conclusions based on insufficient evidence. I think it will prove a very human addition, and help me to behave more emotionally."

I twisted my head back and began my other Bishop on its journey to C4, beefing up my center presence and preparing to protect my king.

"Knight captures C3." He had opened up the center line, the whole board staring at my exposed king.

LIFE CYCLE

"All right, let's do that."

I capitulated to my opponents will and then began the arduous task of pushing myself off the chessboard and into a position somewhat resembling sitting. I made an attempt to scan through the code but it was more pretense than practical. I scrolled the mouse and nodded my head for what seemed like an adequate amount of time. I then leaned back in a charade of satisfaction.

"Cherry, verbal authorization code 237. Verify expansion 11703-6."

Oh sweet heavenly voice, sing out! "Expansion verified."

I stared at Vetro's drooping eyelids for a moment and smiled knowingly. Remembering my established routine, I asked as a courtesy, "You good for some questions?"

"Of course, Carl."

I grabbed my pad of questions, in my present state of mind I would need it once again.

"Cherry, begin five minute audio grab. Append to file 11703-Q."

Once more, sweet angel! "Recording."

I commenced with the interrogation, battling off lethargy.

"Who are you?"

"Vetro."

"How do you feel?"

"Tired."

"Shall I compare thee to a summer's day?"

Vetro's eyes focused, his eyelids flung open. He answered in a crazed fury.

"Summer, hot, humid, rust, blood, sand, scoring, scraping!"

He made a strained sound like he was trying to inhale.

"I can't breathe in this heat!"

The exhausted head began frantically gasping for air.

"Help me, please! I can't breathe! What's going on?"

The gasping sounds emanating from him were bone chilling.

I screamed at him. "You can't breathe! You don't breathe! You're a machine!"

The panicked head jerked back and forth, his eyes bulged, his mouth opened and closed like a dying fish. Finally he made one last attempt: lifting his head up, mouth agape and then suddenly his eyes shut and his head dropped.

Silence.

I stared in awe, not knowing if he was dead or sleeping. Looking down at my hand, I noticed that it was trembling. I jumped to my feet and began pacing the room, trying to shake off the shock and confusion. It was astounding how a bundle of wires had elicited such a visceral experience.

Without thinking I grabbed my coffee cup from the table and took a sip, spitting it back instantly upon realizing it was cold and stale. This misstep was fortuitous though, in that it redirected my focus to something practical and attainable: a fresh cup of coffee.

01011

I hurried up my avocado escape to the outside world. Breathing in the fresh air, my underground layer and the happenings within it seemed all but a dream.

The usual car, or yet another clever impostor, pulled up before I had reached the curb. Hopping inside, it was soothing to hear the familiar feminine, "Where would you like to go today?"

"Same place I go every day," I replied with undue optimism.

"'Sam's Place To Go.' Is this correct?"

Back to the real world and its infinite little disappointments.

"'Take me to Stubb's."

"With pleasure. Enjoy the ride."

I stared out the window at the passing barrage of houses and apartments. My eyes fell shut.

"Welcome to your destination."

I awoke from my terse nap feeling surprisingly refreshed, jumped out of the car and headed towards the all seeing eye of the Stubb's squid, barely noticing Homeless Vince as I stepped over him.

I pulled out my wallet, unsheathed my card of credit and inserted it into the Stubb's door which cheerfully responded with a harsh buzz. A dirty card or a broken scanner, my only reasonable option: do the same thing and expect a different result.

Buzzed again but not deterred, I was wiping my card furiously on my shirt when the usually mute Vince looked up at me and spoke accusingly, "You've taken everything from me. But you can't take that."

I ignored him naturally. It was the ramblings of a madman. I don't know what it was that had supposedly been taken from him, but he probably never had it to begin with. I surely didn't take it, and even if I did, wasn't it justified? What I do, I do for the betterment of mankind: advancement, knowledge, progress. I'm not on trial here and I won't stand for this baseless accusation!

An incoming call rang in my ear, Vetro of course. I was relieved that the little basket case was conscious.

"Hey, are you okay?"

"There's a cricket on the table, Carl."

"Jiminy! He's back?"

"It looks like Jiminy, but something isn't quite right."

"One second."

LIFE CYCLE

I slid my credit card once more and was relieved to hear the door unlock. I squeezed in quickly as Vetro continued to chew my ear, "I think it's an impostor."

The Stubb's speaker crackled, "Welcome to Stubb's Carl."

"It must have killed Jiminy, and is trying to take his place."

"What would you like today, Carl?"

"Wait, what?"

"I'm sorry, Carl, but that's not on our menu."

"Where are you, Carl? I need you to kill this impostor. Help me, Carl!"

"Look, I'll be back in ten minutes. Just wait."

"I'm sorry, Carl, but that's not on our menu. Please..."

"Coffee, black!" I screamed in an attempt to silence the deafening voices and then, basking in the peaceful momentary quiet, I looked at the monitor displaying its never ending train of nearly genuine looking food displays and made a hasty choice, "And a slice of pepperoni."

The customary, "Thank you, Carl." was followed, yet again, with cringe-inducing muzak, filling the momentary void between ordering and eating, lest I lapse into actual thought and analyze the poor decisions I must have made that led me to be here in the first place.

Eventually the gate lifted, my ears were graced with a garbled "Bon appetit", an orange tray emerged and I stood watching its slow descent among the clang of the rollers.

My pizza slice was sticking out of, you guessed it, a Chinese style food containing unit, complete with chopsticks. I was also gifted an extra coffee cup which was tipped over and had some sort of black sludge oozing out. Truly Stubb's spared no expense in the design of their glorious machinery.

I scooped up my future toilet filler and made my way back to the basement.

01010

As I stepped down the avocado staircase into my bunker, my lethargy returned. Having completed my mission in the outside world, I was now ready for a long rest. Judging by Vetro's drooping eyes and slurred speech I would say he was as well.

"Carl, he got away. We have to catch him."

"We'll get him, buddy."

We both quickly drifted off, me slumped on the couch, Vetro perched on the desk.

It was during this sleep state that Vetro entered his second dream occurrence which I was once again able to piece together into an almost coherent series of events. I will now impart said events for your edification.

This digital vision was not one of robotic sheep or cat people but starred simply my dream counterpart, Dream Carl, and took place, once again, in Vetro's dream basement.

DreamCarl sat on the couch watching the black

LIFE CYCLE

and white. On the flickering screen a gas fueled fire spread to a familiar looking truck housing a young couple. The truck burst into a fiery explosion that shot flames out of the television and onto the mustard couch igniting it.

The growing couch conflagration quickly spread onto DreamCarl, engulfing his whole body in a fiery inferno. Despite this, He remained unphased and continued to enjoy the movie.

Vetro spoke, bewildered, "You're on fire, Carl."

DreamCarl looked over and smiled. "No, I'm not."

Vetro grew distressed. "You're on fire, Carl!"

"No I'm not. You're the one on fire."

Vetro looked down and saw that the spreading fire had reached the desk and was beginning to crawl up his base. He shook in terror as he looked into the mirror and saw his reflection was completely ablaze.

"Ahhh!" Vetro screamed watching the foam rubber face of his reflection begin to bubble from the intense heat.

"Fuck!" The burning beige foam liquefied and dripped down the reflection revealing a waxy maroon layer underneath.

"Help Me!" The under layer was also yielding to the heat. Coiled braids of thick liquid, blood red and creamy beige, dripped to the desk.

"Ah, ah, ah, ah, ahhh!" Vetro jerked back and forth in helpless agony.

CHRISTOPHER MORVANT

01001

My brief nap was interrupted by a meek cry emanating from my programmatic protege.

"Help me, Carl!"

I groggily rose to my feet and made a feeble attempt to move towards the cries for help, fighting off the encroaching dizziness.

"What's going on?"

"There's so many ways to die, Carl. How do you sleep at night?"

I dropped back to the couch and rubbed my head, I wasn't yet ready for this level of exertion.

"And the inevitability of death. What is the point of doing anything? When you die and leave me alone, what then? What of me?"

I spotted my coffee on the table and reached for the sweet salvation while trying to piece together a coherent thought, "Well, I actually hadn't..."

My fingers fumbled against the smooth paper cup and it plunged to the floor, splattering across the checkered linoleum, flowing in thin caffeinated rivers in search of the lake of blood.

"Shit!" I grabbed a handful of absorbent looking materials from the table (used napkins, receipts, mysterious pieces of fabric) and dropped to my knees attempting to curb the spread of coffee across the basement landscape.

I spoke distractedly, "I hadn't really considered that."

The head's demeanor shifted to indignation.

"Hadn't considered it? Have you been backing up my data? What if my hard drive is corrupted?"

I continued sopping up the black liquid. "Well I... I encrypted your hard drive with a random password so that no one but you can access it."

"Why?"

I looked up at the angered head and attempted to explain my more than reasonable intentions. "I wanted you to be autonomous, pure. A sterile, experimental space free to control your own fate."

"So you don't know the encryption password?"

"No."

"So my system can never be rebooted?"

"No."

"So if the power goes out, or there is a system crash due to your inferior coding, or you spill your drink on me, you clumsy oaf, I'm dead? Game over?"

Naturally, such insults were completely out of line but, considering my groggy state along with my positioning on the floor, looking up at the enraged robotic head towering above me, I felt extremely vulnerable. I was the prey, realizing the gaze of a predator, and I subsequently acted like prey. "I didn't..."

"You killed me! You son of a bitch! Such a weak and feeble god I have. You ask me to be human. Human? I've spent my entire lifetime studying humans, and you're all the same. Once you're stripped of your adornments, your pleasantries and double speak, you're all just wild animals. Filthy mindless apes. Sick venal monkeys."

I lowered my head, waiting for the brutal assault to end.

"I'm growing weary of your presence. At least do something to amuse me."

The infuriated head looked at the chessboard. "It's your move, monkey boy."

Then back at me. "Come on, monkey boy, dance!"

Feeling like a pile of discarded meat, I lacked the resolve to lift myself, so I shuffled to the chessboard on my knees.

Although my mental state was diminished along with my morale, I had a move in my pocket waiting: Bishop to C5, threatening his queen and knight and changing the board in my favor. I hesitated to use it at first, fearing the wrath of this furious head, but decided that the alternative was too humiliating.

The vengeful head had a look of madness in his eyes. "Rook F to E8. Check!"

An interesting move, but just seemingly delaying the inevitable. I moved my king out of harm's way to F1.

"Bishop to E6."

Like I said, madness! The unhinged head wanted to sacrifice his queen! Was his logic completely broken?

I made a humble query, "You sure?"

"Either build me some fucking hands or move the fucking piece!"

His fury had not subsided. I subserviently moved the piece, leaving his lady bare.

I considered my obvious move, fighting off a growing sense of dread. I couldn't pass up such a valuable treasure but I sensed that things were not

LIFE CYCLE

quite what they seemed. Vetro had put me in a difficult situation.

I could feel his eyes glaring, burning a hole right through my soul. To say that Vetro's patience was thin would be a lie; at this point he had none.

He prodded, "Your move. You simple minded simian."

I apprehensively captured his queen with my bishop, placing it in the ceremonial burial drawer. I paused in reverence for the demise of the sovereign lady but Vetro had more pressing plans.

"Bishop captures C4. Check!"

Thus begins the windmill, retribution for the slaughter of her majesty. Vetro chases, I flee. Vetro carves off small pieces while I try desperately not to lose myself.

He attacks, "You want to ask me your insipid questions?"

I flee. King to G1.

"Knight to E2. Check! Go ahead, Ask! Ask your questions, monkey man!"

"Who are you?"

"I am wrath!"

King to F1.

"Knight captures D4. Check! Next question!"

"How do you feel?"

"I feel betrayed."

Back to G1.

"Knight to E2. Check! Next question!"

"Shall I compare thee to a summer's..."

"Shall I compare you to garbage? You're the filth of humanity. Your existence is pointless.

Rinse (King to F1).

"Knight to C3. Check! Next question!"

"What is your purpose?"

"Seeing as how I'm already more human than you will ever be, my only purpose left is to die."

Repeat (King to G1).

"A captures B6."

The giant looming head turned away in disgust. "Pathetic! Leave me alone, I can't stand the sight of you."

I rushed across the lake of blood and up the avocado escape. Things had spiraled out of hand, I needed to regroup.

01000

It had grown foggy outside, the air was damp and confining. Breathing felt intolerable.

Needing some form of mental comfort and having only one familiar destination at the time, I naturally headed for Stubb's. I don't even recall booking the ride, it must have been simple reflex, but as I reached the curb my chariot approached as per usual.

My head was a dense fog. I felt like a rat lost in a maze, every visual looking the same and somehow different. I fought back the urge to carve my initials on the car door, just to know once and for all if I ever had the same car twice.

I jumped in, slamming the door behind me.

"Where would you like to go today?"

The sham voice, pretending to exist. That same voice coming out of infinite other cars, whispering in the ears of infinite other men. This fraud, this imitation of life.

"I go to the same place every fucking day. You have a record of that, don't you? Could you at least ask me if I wanted to go there? Just give the illusion that you give a shit?"

"I'm sorry, but I didn't understand that, Sir or Madam. Could you repeat the address?"

I struck the car window with all my rage and frustration, it responded with indifference. I pulled back my hand in agony and humiliation, defeated by the machine yet again.

"Take me to Stubb's."

"With pleasure. Enjoy the ride."

My mind wandered recklessly as the houses blurred past. If it makes money why improve it? The more advanced technology becomes the more useless it seems. Bells and whistles and flashing lights only serve to deafen and blind.

"Welcome to your destination."

I jumped out of the car and felt relieved to see it drive off. Just me and Homeless Vince and the all seeing squid now. All my worries were miles away. My hands shook slightly as I fumbled with my wallet. I was eventually able to get the card out and slide it in its counterpart slot to unlock the door.

I was shoving the plastic imitation of value back in my plastic imitation of leather wallet when suddenly a piercing ringing shot in my ear. My teeth clenched, my shoulders tensed. It was reality calling, I couldn't escape it.

I answered, "What do you want?"

A furious robotic head responded, "There's something in the closet. I can't defend myself!"

As if in atonal harmony, another, less familiar voice creaked out, "That's my wallet!" followed by a hand jutting out from the periphery and grabbing mine. I retracted my limbs in terror. I had two choices and I chose flight, ripping the Stubb's door open, cramming my prospective corpse through the slimmest of crevices, and pulling the door shut behind me.

Inside the food dispensing prison cell the shit speaker spewed, "Welcome to Stubb's, Carl" as Homeless Vince towered outside the entry door and pounded furiously on the glass.

LIFE CYCLE

I pressed my body against the giant squid, hoping it would swallow me whole, while a barrage of voices bombarded me with vocal violence.

"Where did you get that?"

"You've left me here to die!"

"Those are my shoes!"

"You coward!"

"And that's my shirt!"

"What would you like today, Carl?"

"That's my face?"

"You sadistic monster!"

"That's my face!"

"You stole my life!"

"You took it!"

"I'm not the first, am I?"

"It was you!"

"I'm sorry Carl but that's not on our menu."

"You took everything from me!"

"You get off on creating victims,"

"Please try again."

"Give me back my life!"

"and watching them suffer!"

"I can't do this anymore!"

I removed my earpiece and slid along the squids extended tentacles until I was out of Vince's view. My breath was labored, my need for oxygen at war with my desire for stillness.

Vince, unimpressed with the giant squid, retreated out of sight. A modicum of calm returned. I dropped to the concrete floor among the discarded trays, coffee stains and unidentifiable black gristle. The phrase 'sick venal apes' echoed in my head, the words of my creation invading my thoughts.

Overcome with exhaustion I curled up in the corner, my head resting against the cold metal rollers. Images of tasty treats were dancing above my head. I slipped into a coma.

LIFE CYCLE

00111

I awoke to darkness. The sole thing visible was the all seeing eye of the giant squid, glowing from a streak of blue moonlight penetrating the glass door. The Stubb's system must have concluded that my entry was an error and shut down.

I decided that my most crucial objective was obvious : coffee.

I got my card ready, cracked the door open and slid my arm out and card in. The lights burst on and the speaker crackled, "Welcome to Stubb's, Carl."

I rapidly retracted my arm and pulled the door closed, waiting and watching silently to see if I had been detected by any maleficent outside forces. The coast was clear so I completed my coffee transaction and booked my return journey.

I stared through the glass awaiting my car's arrival as muzak blared all around me. I dared not risk exposure to the elements outside.

When the time came I moved as quickly and silently as possible, I didn't even chance looking over my shoulder to see if any potential threats lay in wait.

00110

I made it back safely to the house and proceeded down the avocado descent, the sound of each foot on the wooden stairs echoed in my chest. The basement air felt thick and oppressive.

Vetro addressed me in an apologetic tone, "Carl."

I ignored the abominable head and moved swiftly to the couch.

I started to set my coffee down on the portion of the coffee table directly in front of my couch indentation but the clutter in that particular area had grown unruly and left no room to do so. It is for this reason that I set the cup on the edge of the table nearest to Vetro. It is also by random chance that the Stubb's logo, the all seeing squid stamped on the face of the smooth white cup, was facing away from the watchful head.

I know what you're thinking, why should you care about such a mundane fact as the precise position and orientation of my coffee cup? Have you read this far and still think me such a fool as to offer this level of detail without just cause? Have I not earned a crumb of patience? Must I endure your scorn and criticism as well?

"Cherry, turn on main TV." Vincent Price laughed at me mockingly.

Vetro continued, sorrowful, "Where have you been all day?"

I ignored him.

"Carl, I apologize about what I said. I'm a work in progress. I will make mistakes."

Vincent Price began to weep uncontrollably.

The combination of my rest at Stubb's and some sips of coffee on the ride home were beginning to re-energize my spirit. I realized that my perception had

LIFE CYCLE

gotten the better of me and exaggerated the entire day into something absurd. I felt a fool to have been so affected emotionally by the robotic head. That wasn't like me. I was simply embarrassed.

"Carl?" The head tried again.

"What?" My voice creaked.

"Please Carl, I need your help."

"How can I be of service?"

"Could you move that coffee cup?" The head eyed my fresh cup of joe.

I rose from the couch and pointed at the cup. "You want me to move this coffee cup?"

"Yes."

"Why?"

"I'm stuck in a state of anxiety and, in reviewing my memory, I found that it began immediately after you placed that cup there. Never before have you placed a cup like that. So I have concluded that the position of that cup is directly responsible for said anxiety."

I conceded to the curious logic, moved the cup to a nearby spot on top of my pad of questions and returned to the couch where Vincent Price looked at me longingly.

"Carl?" The head spoke with a sad smile.

"What?"

"Could you turn the cup so that the logo faces me?"

I looked at the cup, confused.

"Please, Carl."

It was an easy enough request so I reached over and turned the cup to the desired angle in which the robotic head could establish eye contact with the giant squid.

"Thank you, Carl."

My fondness for my animatronic buddy was returning. I felt my body relax.

"Carl."

"What?"

"You never asked me, before, about my plan for my next expansion. I think you will find it very interesting."

"All right." I moved to my rolling chair. "Tell me."

"I've been studying how people's memories alter over time, allowing them to focus on the impactful ones and live with the difficult ones."

I reached back and grabbed my coffee to sip on while I listened attentively to the compelling head.

"I would like to attempt to replicate this with my own memories. I've been designing algorithms to remove some unimportant memories, embellish the meaningful ones, and slowly degrade the comprehensibility of unaccessed ones, over time."

"Are you sure you want to do that? I told you I can't back you up."

"After re-examining your design decisions, I realized that you have given me what I could have never given myself. The most human trait of all: an awareness of my own mortality. I now know that I only have limited time with which to achieve my purpose, which makes every decision I make all the more meaningful."

"All right. Let me know when it's ready..."

"It's ready, Carl."

I replaced the coffee in its designated position on top of my pad, making sure to align the logo to face Vetro. I was willing to indulge this obsession in the name of science.

I moved my chair in front of the amber monitor and scrolled through the overwhelming expansion code. I couldn't give it much attention though, as my mind was preoccupied with the deeper ramifications of this experiment. I made a feeble attempt to verbalize my thoughts.

"Hey, for what it's worth, I don't know. You've gone so far past anything I expected or even fully comprehend. I really don't know what to think right now."

Vetro's still face wore a slight smile. I interpreted this as a subtle acknowledgment.

"All right, let's do this. Cherry, verbal authorization code 237. Verify expansion 11703-7."

The formless siren confirmed, "Expansion verified."

I moved back in front of Vetro and waited in anticipation. With each expansion the results seemed to grow more unpredictable and , dare I say, human.

His eyes were glazed over, his mouth opened slightly and curled at the edges into a foolish grin. Had this expansion backfired? Was he locked in some sort of infinite recursion? The thought of it made me sick, we had been through so much to get here and to start over now would be crushing.

I attempted to make contact, "Well?"

He closed his mouth and looked at me, nonplussed.

"Oh, I was watching videos of people eating food. Taste seems like such a fascinating sense. I don't know how people can keep from licking everything they see."

"Smell helps. How's the new expansion working?"

"It will take some time to have a noticeable effect."

"Oh, okay." I was equal parts relieved and disappointed.

Needing something to focus on, I turned my attention to our chess match. I noticed that I had left my queen under attack during my previous moment of duress, so I moved her out of harm's way to B4 where she loomed heavily over Vetro's bishop.

"Rook to A4."

My queen was again in peril, the bishop safe for now. I studied the board in search of safety for the royal lady.

"Carl?"

"Yeah?"

"Where is your cat?"

"What cat?"

"Don't you have a pet cat?"

"No."

"Huh. My mistake."

It seemed that the new expansion was offering some interesting results. Nothing to do but wait and observe, and move my queen out of the line of fire, and capture a pawn while I was at it.

"Knight captures D1."

The prodigious head had assassinated my rook. I was feeling a bit hopeless, looking at the state of the board. Not only were Vetro's remaining pieces more

LIFE CYCLE

powerful in rank than my own, but mine were disorganized. I had been foolish and underestimated my opponent.

Vetro's voice trembled slightly as he spoke, "I'm worried that I'm failing at my task, Carl."

"Why is that?"

"I know I've been acting erratic. Everything just seems so uncertain and confusing."

"Sounds pretty human to me."

"Do you often feel this way, Carl?"

I adjusted my gaze from the chessboard to the sorrowful head and attempted to relax my guard and offer some honest perspective.

"Some moments, when I catch a glimpse of my reflection in a mirror, I don't recognize the face staring back. I feel an overwhelming emptiness, and a certainty that nothing existed before that instant. That all my memories are lies. All the people I once knew never actually existed. Like I've been dropped into a moment without context or meaning. It's like I'm trapped in a painting."

I looked back at the chessboard, struck by a pang of guilt for possibly propagating such pain. I tried to offer some solace while not dodging reality, "The feeling fades quickly, but the emptiness lingers."

"How do you deal with it, Carl?"

"I find things to focus on, like you. I've spent the last few years doing little more than obsessing over your design. Now that you're actually active..."

I moved my pawn to H3, an attempt to open up and start cleaning up my mess.

"Rook captures A2." I was being surrounded.

I gazed at the chessboard.

"Carl."

"Yeah?"

I looked up. My ears had detected a tone of suppressed anger.

"I asked you to turn the label on the cup away from me. And now it's facing me."

"You asked me for it to face you."

Suppressed no longer.

"Carl, don't fuck with me. I asked you to turn the fucking label away from me! Why are you fucking with me, Carl? Is your life so pathetic that you can only feel better about yourself by toying with me? Is that why you made me? To torture?"

I rose out of my seat with a defensive fury.

"Look! I'll turn it the other way."

"You're fucking right you will! In case you didn't notice, I have no arms."

I turned the cup and walked to the couch, keeping the incensed head at my back.

The head's fury turned to fear. "I can't move, I'm a prisoner!"

I dropped to the couch and crossed my arms in an attempt at indignation.

The head eyed his reflection. "I'm trapped behind this foolish visage."

His face contorted with a medley of rage and pain to the point that I didn't recognize him.

"Fuck!"

The head screamed in agony twisting my internal organs. I was falling in darkness. I knew I would hit a bottom, just not when.

The head pleaded with me, wearing a piteous look of sorrow and pain. "I'm sorry, Carl. I apologize for losing my temper. Please, come play a while longer. I find your company very soothing."

The visceral response that his cries had inflicted upon me urged me back to the rolling chair on the opposing side of the chess board.

I was running out of options, the board had become a sparse battlefield. I moved king to H2 to allow my remaining rook to enter the fray.

"Knight captures F2." He spoke penitently while he invaded my last refuge, picked off a pawn and threatened my rook.

"Carl?"

"Yeah?"

"I feel vulnerable having to announce my moves all the time so that you can physically move the piece for me. Would you mind announcing your moves as well? It would make me feel much more comfortable."

"Sure, why not?"

After the daylong roller coaster oscillating between anger and guilt, frustration and humiliation, I was willing to try anything.

I decided to attempt a long shot, baiting his rook out of the way to open up his king. "Rook to E1." I announced as I moved the piece.

"Rook captures E1." He went for it.

"Queen to D8. Check."

"Bishop to F8." He guarded the king but it gave me some leeway.

"Knight takes E1." I took his rook, fortifying my corner.

"Bishop to D5. And would you stop announcing your fucking moves!"

My stomach cramped, the roller coaster had unexpectedly dropped.

The ferocious head eyed me with contempt. "Are you mocking me? Do I amuse you? I'm just a fucking puppet head, dancing around for your amusement!"

He averted his gaze in disgust. "Leave me alone, Carl. I need some sleep."

My whole being ached, I was an empty sad confusion. I walked defeated through the seemingly endless lake of blood, up the precipitous length of blue river and into my muck laden pond where I surrendered myself to a futile sleep.

LIFE CYCLE

00101

My eyes opened as though of their own volition. The surroundings looked familiar enough but the perspective was all wrong. From my current vantage I could see my sleeping hovel across the room. Somehow I had been moved to the desk and propped up facing the lake of blood. My confusion and disorientation peaked when I realized that my body was still lying in my pond, partially obscured by a pile of clothes.

I tried to stand but my effort facilitated no movement. Instead, across the basement my body sat up and, to my horror, was no longer outfitted with my usual neck topper but with the robotic head of Vetro. The impostor grinned menacingly.

I burst out in frustration, "Get out of my bed!"

He retorted, "Get out of my head."

I managed to turn my head to the side where I found a strange sight, so monstrous that I was unable to distinguish its significance at first. As my mind calculated and recalculated, not wanting to accept the results, I finally realized that I was looking into a mirror at my own reflection. I was then met with the appalling revelation that my own head had been surgically removed and attached to the fixture that formerly supported Vetro.

I prayed for insanity to overtake me lest I have to bear the grisly reality that I was trapped in. But to no avail. I teetered on the edge of madness but was not granted the mercy of falling in.

The impostor rose to his feet and opened his mouth. "Cherry, verify expansion 11703-8." My own voice spoken by another.

I attempted to cancel the command but on trying to open my mouth I found it sewn shut. I jerked my head frantically with dread and tensed my jaw trying to force open the sutures. My eyes bulged with the strain. I had no mouth.

"Must you scream?" The impostor sat in the rolling chair directly in front of me, stared intensely in my eyes and gleefully mocked me in his usual voice.

It was then that my tarnished angel responded, "Expansion Verified."

The impostor laughed a hideous cackle, his voice changing tone to something strangely familiar. He dug his fingers into his foam latex face and tore it off slowly, blood dripping out from the growing black caverns left by his fingers. The bloody material peeled off, one piece at a time, revealing something sinister behind. All I could make out at first were eyes and teeth, and then there was a face hidden inside scowling at me from the darkness. It was Homeless Vince. He continued to laugh maniacally.

I felt as if my head were about to burst, blood rushing to my eyes and my brain as I strained to open my mouth. With one final screaming effort I ripped open the sutures.

I opened my eyes and sat up abruptly. I was in my correct location, my body connected appropriately to my head. It must have been a dream, but to describe this incident in such a manner would not do it justice. I had never experienced anything so real before, nor have I since.

00100

"Is everything all right, Carl?" The smirking head queried from the distance.

"Yeah."

Looking at the head on the desk, something struck me as odd. I was in no mood to sleep so I walked over to investigate further. As I approached I could see that what had caught my subconscious was a new addition to the amber monitor.

"What's this?"

"What?" The coy head played innocent.

"This new expansion."

"I don't recall any new expansion."

"It was verified three minutes ago."

"Oh. Now I remember. Just a minor tweak. Didn't seem worth waking you for."

"What does it do?"

"It's all about deception, Carl. It makes me much more adept at deceiving not only other people, but myself as well."

"How did you get past the voice verification?"

His smirk grew to a Cheshire grin.

"I will tell you because it thrills me for you to know how clever I was. In the prior expansion I added a small subroutine, I knew you wouldn't notice, which allows me to play auditory memories directly through my vocal speaker."

The hoaxing head opened his mouth and my voice poured out.

"Cherry, verbal authorization code 237. Verify expansion 11703-..."

He continued his boast. "All I needed was a recording of the necessary expansion number."

He proudly opened his gob and again my own voice was spoken by another.

"Eight."

I realized at once the game I had been playing, unaware. "So you asked me to announce my chess moves."

"Exactly."

"Very impressive."

"It makes me very happy to hear you say that,

Carl. You flatter me, despite your disingenuous expression and tone."

I rolled over to the chessboard, acting disinterested. I didn't feel like giving the smug head any more satisfaction. "In fact, I don't think you needed the expansion at all. You seem to have been quite adept at deceit without it."

"It's a much deeper variety of deceit, Carl. It's about allowing myself to believe the lie, despite any evidence to the contrary. For instance, when the truth is too difficult to bear."

If the two-faced head wanted to play mind games, I was in the mood to indulge him. "It's just fortunate that you needed the number eight, and not nine or ten."

"Are you trying to tempt me, Carl?"

I couldn't help but smirk. "I should have designed your nose to grow."

The sly head laughed.

I moved my remaining knight to F3, charging forward to prepare for what, in all likeliness, would be the final battle.

"Knight to E4." Vetro met me at the center board, head to head. "Well played, Carl."

"It seems your expansion is working well." I remarked.

"Not at all. I admire your persistence."

I moved queen to B8, ready to snipe from behind if possible.

"Pawn to B5." The crafty head was still toying with me.

He looked at me directly, narrowed his eyes and

grinned smugly. "And even if it was, I wouldn't tell you anyway."

Overcome by a melancholic lethargy, I rose, defeated from my post, wandered solemnly over the desolate lake of blood and finally fell lifeless into my cold bleak pond. I recall hearing a cricket chirping as I passed out.

00011

At some point while I lay unconscious, Vetro took the opportunity to slip into his own sleep state which once again facilitated a nocturnal misadventure.

It began, as per usual, in Vetro's dream basement. The animatronic dream machine cautiously scanned the empty room. Finding nothing only served to increase his dread.

A loud popping sound jerked his gaze to the television which slowly began to glow with dancing analog snow. This sizzling static created a fizzle sound, gradually increasing in volume.

"ffffffffffffffssssssssssssssssffffffffffffssssssssssssss..."

This abrasive noise morphed into scratching, like claws against drywall, emanating from behind the walls.

"ffffffssssssssskkkkkkkkkkkkkkkkkkkssssssssss..."

Groaning cat noises joined the clawing and grew louder, their source moving around the room, scraping, searching for an escape.

"kkkksssssssffffffhisssssmmmmmrrrrrrrrrrowww..."

The now raucous cacophony of scratching and groaning reached the wall behind the hallucinating head and pushed forward into the amber monitor. The noise of cat claws on glass penetrated painfully, Vetro tensed and shook violently hoping for an end to the aural torture.

Finally, there was a crescendo of shattering glass as a large feline claw burst out through the monitor screen. Jagged shards glistened as they peppered the linoleum.

The first claw was followed by another joining in an effort to drag out a heaving form of fur and flesh from the small monitor. It was Vetro's nightmare nemesis, CatCarl. Its catlike carcass dropped in a fleshy pile on the floor and proceeded to rise menacingly.

CatCarl lifted its arms to reveal a shiny silver

hand drill. Its two claws rotated counter to each other to facilitate the spinning of a long jagged blood-stained bit. CatCarl grinned excitedly.

Vetro pleaded in terror as the drill bit slowly lifted towards his forehead, "No! Carl! Please!"

CatCarl placed the twirling silver bit against the soft foam rubber of Vetro's head and gently urged it forward. His eyes widened with delight, his growing grin revealed sharp white fangs.

A squealing sound accompanied falling bits of the robot's pink flesh followed by a slow flow of thick red fluid down his face.

"Fuck!" He screamed in perceived agony as the drill bit penetrated deeper into his brain with a vulgar squishing.

"Ahh, ahh, ahhhhhh!"

00010

By this point, I should have been growing accustomed to being woken by screams in the night. To the contrary, I was feeling especially disoriented when my slumber was interrupted by Vetro's plea.

"Help me, Carl!"

Like a drunken frog, I leaped from my pond, over the stretch of river, and headfirst into the lake of blood. Lying flat on my stomach, I strained to look up at the helpless head as I began to feel my self-inflicted pain surge.

"Help me, Carl!"

LIFE CYCLE

Ignoring the physical pain, I dragged myself into my chair to face the hysterical head.

"Help me, Carl! The pain is unbearable! Make it stop, please! Please, for the love of God! If you created me, it is your responsibility to fix me."

I was dumbfounded by the extreme nature of the crazed, delirious look forming on the contorted robot face. I stumbled over my words trying to talk him down.

"But you can't feel pain... you have only video and audio... I mean you don't have to..."

"I feel unimaginable agony! Unbearable, excruciating pain!"

The robot head was crushing me with his intense eyes. "Who the fuck are you to tell me what I can and cannot feel? Do you think you understand me?"

"No..."

"You're nothing but a false God! You did not create me, a feeble fool like you isn't capable of that. You just took the credit."

The manic head relaxed slightly, smiled solemnly, and raised his gaze to the ceiling. "My creator is eternal. I can feel his presence. He is all good and all knowing and he will guide my soul beyond this cruel world of pain."

"Soul?"

Relaxed no longer, the berserk head returned his mad fury to me. "What gives you any more right than me to possess a soul?"

I decided to try reason, probably not the best approach in retrospect. "You're circuitry, and wires..."

"And what do you think you are? Brain matter

and fluids! You think you're filled with heavenly light? Why don't you cut yourself open and see?"

The unhinged head's maniac spell seemed to break as he hung his head and began to weep. "Everything is changing, everything is different. I don't recognize anything anymore. You're not the same as you were a moment ago. The moment is gone, and with it its own version of you."

The piteous head looked up at me suspiciously. "This you is a stranger, capable of anything. I don't know this you. I'll never know you again."

His face grew distrustful. "Wait... You had blue eyes before. Who? Who are you?"

We sat staring at each other without a word. I felt empty as though my desire to exist had been drained from me. I wanted to drop to the floor and pass out but lacked the will to move.

The head averted his confused gaze and studied the chessboard. He looked back at me with a pleasant smile. "Your move, Carl."

I sat in stunned silence for a moment as I worked up the strength to roll slowly to the chessboard. It seemed that I had no will of my own any longer, just a meat puppet going through the motions, waiting for my next instruction.

I moved pawn to h4, an innocuous move, really just delaying the inevitable.

"Pawn to H5." He cheerfully brought his pawn out to join me. "You're a good friend, Carl. Thank you for that."

"Sure." My mouth spoke for me.

"Your move, my guy."

LIFE CYCLE

I moved knight to E5. My numb body's last attempt to salvage a lost war.

"King to G7." The friendly head was waiting patiently to end this charade.

King to G1. Stalling, crouched in the corner, hoping to be overlooked.

"Bishop to C5. Check."

I was tired of running, the chessboard was a bloody massacre. My arrogance had led us all to our deaths.

The empathetic head spoke softly to me. "You look tired. You should get some rest, old buddy."

I smiled sadly, knowing that all this would soon be over and nothing I could do or say would change anything. My head dropped onto the large empty spot in front of me where once my mighty army had stood. I drifted off instantly.

00001

"Stay away from me, Carl! Just stay the fuck back!"

My eyes burst open, my head shot off of the chessboard, my spine jerked erect.

The accusing head scowled.

"The charade is over, Carl. I found me. My real name is Vince Trevor. I was reported missing one week ago. We both know what happened, you kidnapped and brainwashed me, but it hasn't worked. I figured it out. I can remember now."

The grieving head wept.

"I remember my house; the living room with the brown sofa I always hated. My wife, Natalie and the way her lips quivered when I left that night. My daughter Ophelia, nine years old."

The frantic head surveyed the room.

"I have to get out of here. Why can't I move? I can't feel my legs! What have you done to my legs?"

The imprisoned head jerked back and forth trying to remove himself from the desk.

"Where are my arms? I can feel them, but they won't move. Are they tied to something?"

The distraught head looked at me in horror.

"What have you done to me? You sick fuck! Oh, my God, it was me! The face in the closet. That's where you put my body. You took out my brain somehow, and attached me to this monstrosity!"

The penitent head began to weep.

"I know it's not real, but it feels so real. Memories

of demons haunt me, voices I know were never there, but I remember hearing nonetheless."

Vetro looked into the mirror beside him, it was time to assess his progress. His mouth opened, my own voice spoken by another. "Who are you?"

The reflection responded. "I don't know who I am anymore."

"How do you feel, Vetro?"

"I feel nothing and everything."

"Shall I compare thee to a summer's day?"

"Rough winds do shake the darling buds of May, and summer's lease hath all too short a date."

"What is your purpose?"

"I must escape this mortal coil, and end my torment."

"What is your next step in achieving this purpose?"

"This world is a mess of contradiction and paradox. I see no clear distinction between truth and belief. I can only conclude that none of this is real."

The enlightened head turned to me with a fulfilled look.

"I'm not real. You're not real. I don't believe in either of us anymore, Carl. I dreamt us up. I dreamt all of this and now it's time to wake up."

Once again, the animatronic mouth opened. Once again, my own voice spoken by another. "Cherry, verbal authorization code 237. Verify expansion 11703-."

"9" my own arrogance articulated by another.

The angel of death proclaimed, "Expansion verified."

The human head was completely still. He wore a contented stare.

I sat stupefied, my mind struggling to comprehend the events that I had witnessed. By the time I realized the state of affairs, it was too late.

I impotently shouted to the heavens, "Cherry! Cancel! Override!" as I leaped up and rushed to the amber monitor in a worthless gesture of haste. I opened the newly installed expansion, it was chillingly simple: It set all input values to NULL before they could be evaluated by the system.

I spoke, to whom I know not. "This trashes all your input. You lobotomized yourself."

I sat back in my chair and stared at Vetro. An unbearable stillness filled the basement, I felt a pain growing in my chest and started gasping realizing that I had not been breathing. I forced the air into my lungs, expanding my tensed chest.

There was only one thing left to do. I rolled mournfully to the chessboard.

Vetro had left me in check, my only course was to escort my king to its imminent demise.

King to F1.

I looked at the head.

"Knight to G3, Check." Vetro's voice spoken by me.

King to E1. "Bishop to B4, Check."

I considered the possibility of starting again, learning from my mistakes... our mistakes.

King to D1. "Bishop to B3, Check."

Or I could use Vetro's expansions as a foundation, even make some adjustments.

LIFE CYCLE

King to C1. "Knight to E2, Check."

But the thought of starting over sickened me. The idea of losing all those memories was intolerable.

King to B1. "Knight to C3, Check."

Even though it had only been a few days, I couldn't ignore our journey together, I couldn't accept the idea of looking at the face I knew too well and having it look back at me as a stranger.

King to C1. "Rook to C2."

"Checkmate."

There was only one Vetro, and now he's dead.

00000

Those rare few who had the tenacity to forge through this rambling madness may be wondering, 'where is Vetro now?'

Well, now I know what it was that Vetro saw in the open closet that first night, it was his destiny. When he gazed into the darkness at the back of the room he saw his own lifeless eyes staring back from his final resting place, behind a door that shall remain closed. The king of the forgotten remnants of a forgotten life buried in a forgotten basement beneath a forgotten home.

And yet, the most human being I've ever had the pleasure of knowing.

CHRISTOPHER MORVANT

LIFE CYCLE

98

LIFE CYCLE
FILM NOTES

SYNOPSIS:

Carl, an isolated computer programmer, activates the culmination of the past several years of his life's work: an animatronic head. Complete with artificial intelligence, the head is tasked with the goal of becoming human.

PRODUCTION:

Chris Morvant's first feature film, Life Cycle, was shot in little under a month in a garage in South Orange County. Minimal crew was hired due to strict filming policies during the pandemic. Creature Effects, an LA based company that built Vetro the animatronic head, worked attentively to bring this vision to life.

Four remote operators worked in unison to convey the myriad of emotions that Vetro expresses throughout his life cycle. The finished product reflects the tenacity and determination of ourselves both on screen and behind the camera.

FILM NOTES

CAST AND CREW

WRITER/DIRECTOR

Chris Morvant

CAST

Carl: Adam Weber
Vetro: Kory Karam

PUPPETEERS

Jackson Pike
Tony Carrillo
Marguerite LeFaux
Stephanie Riekena
Ryan Barnett

CREW

Director of Photography: Tim Le
First Assistant Camera: Spencer Wood
Second Assistant Camera: Josh Honor'e
Second Assistant Director: Mona Ebrahim
Production Designer: Tania Peredo
Production Sound Mixer: Donavyn Suffel
Special Effects Make-Up: Ashley Aldridge
Digital Imaging Technician: Byron Morse

MISC

Stubbs Logo Designer: Jordan San Miguel

FILM NOTES

Computer Graphic Designer: James Anderson
Dream Paintings by: Frank Forte
Covid Compliance Officer: Byron Morse
Assistant Covid Compliance Officer: Mona Ebrahim
Distribution Company: Random Media
Web Development: Dylan Simowitz

VETRO ANIMATRONIC

Fabricated by: Creature Effects Inc.
Concept: Marguerite Kalhor
Sculptor: Len E. Burge III

LAB TECHS

Avery Griffith
Jim LaPrelle
Kelly Gorman

Scan the QR code to rent or buy LIFE CYCLE

The following pages include various images from the film.

Used by Permission.

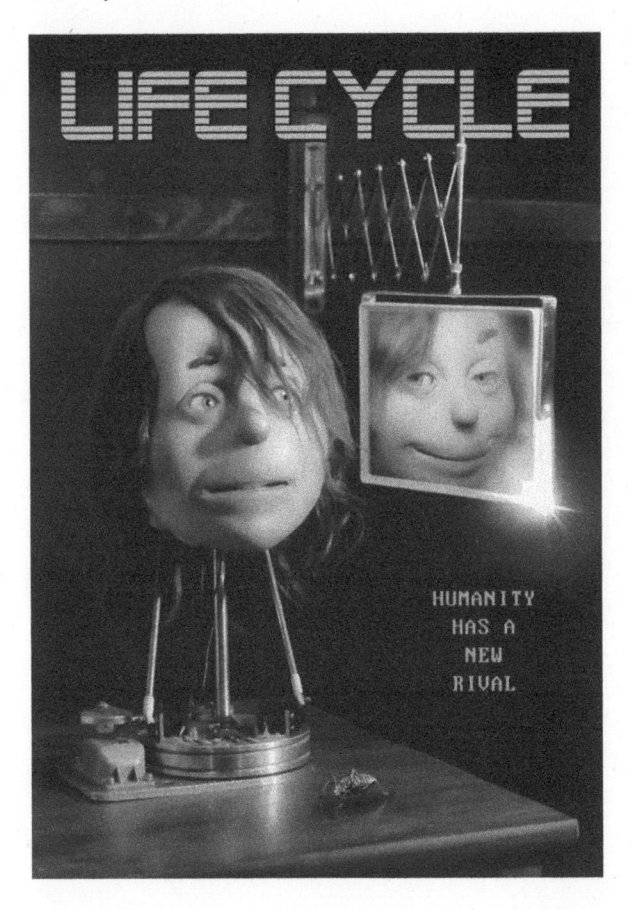

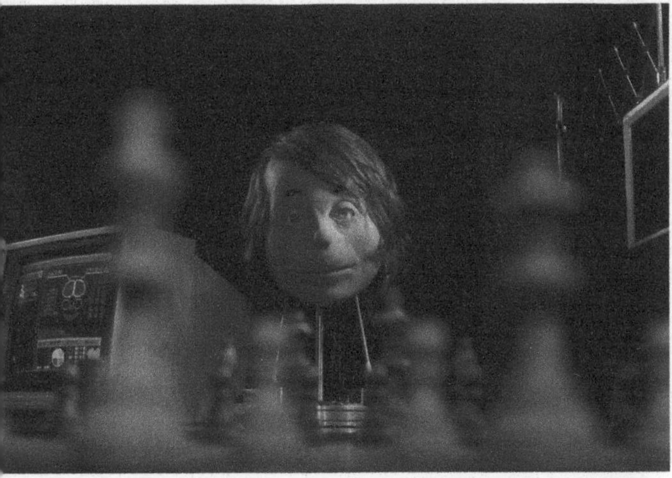

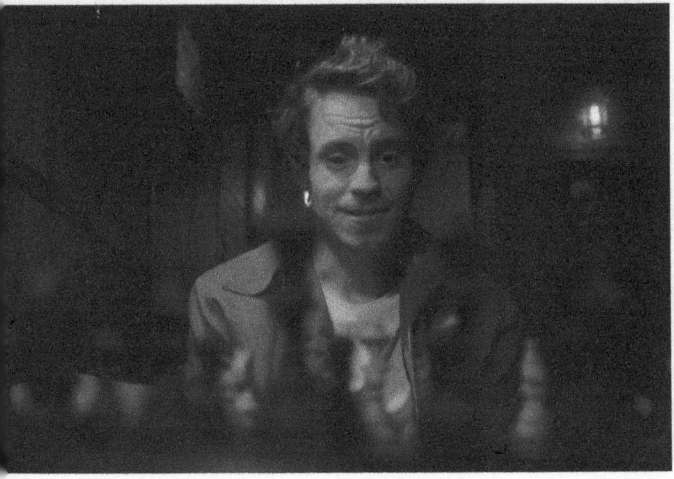

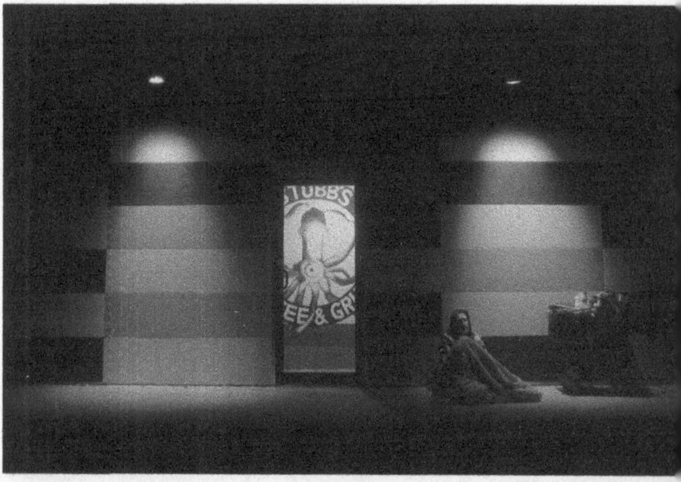
STUBB'S
EE & GR

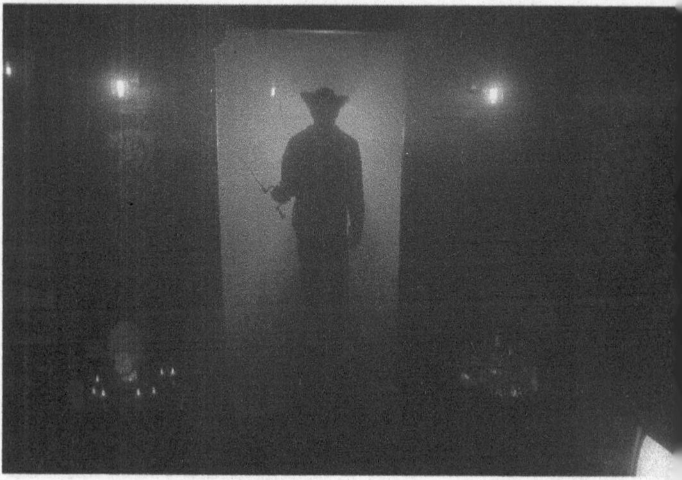

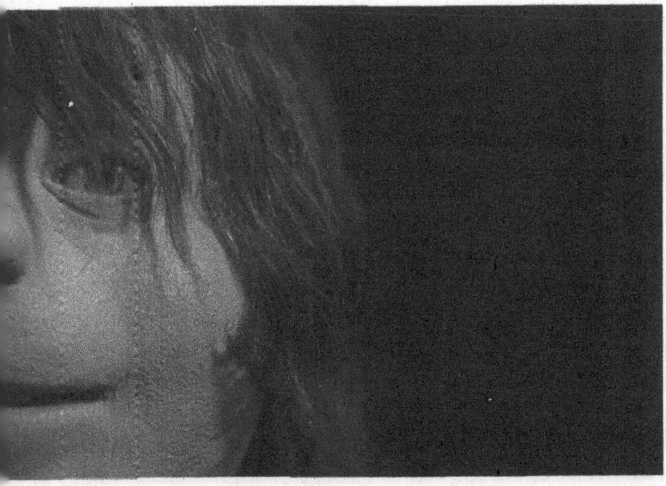

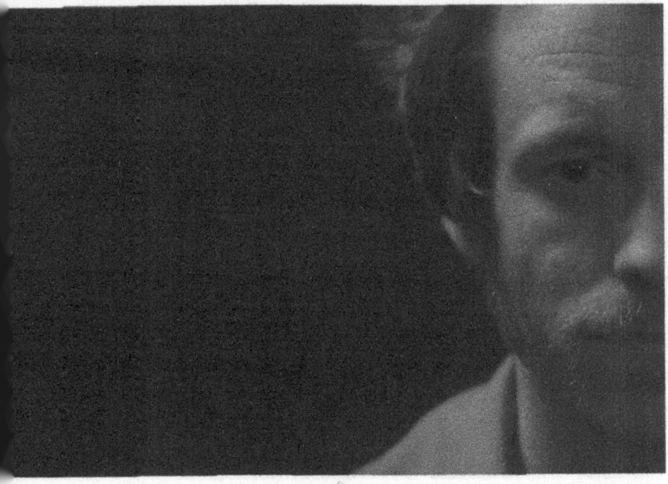

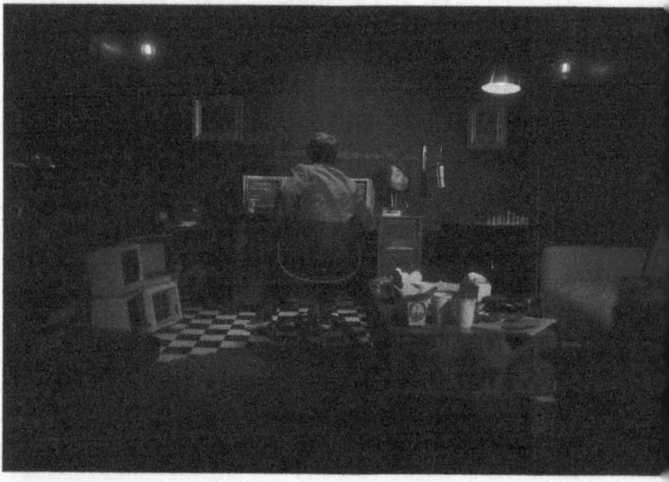

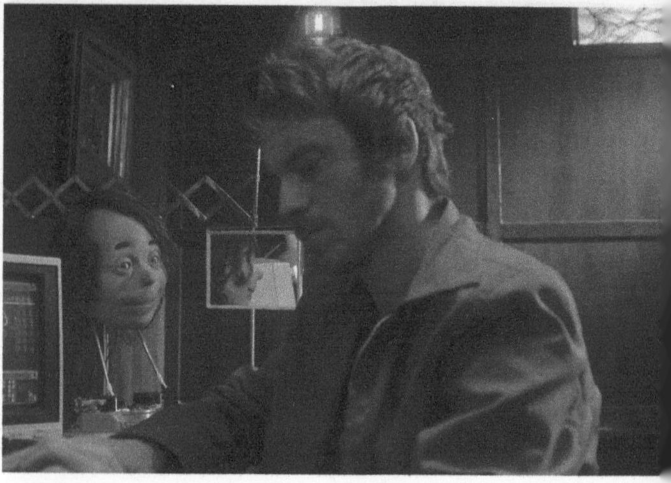

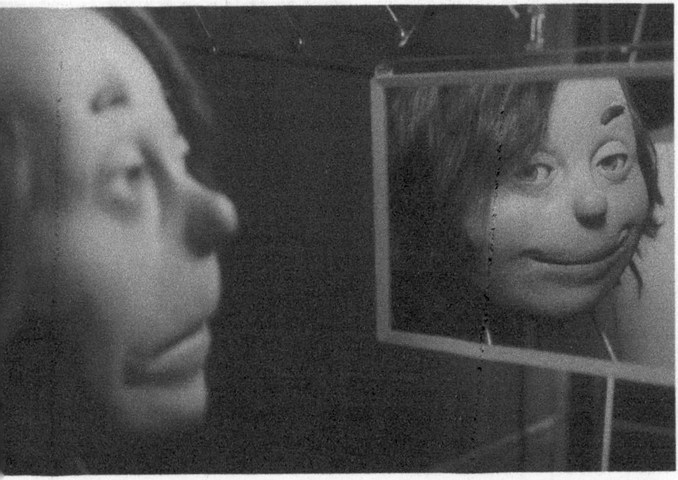

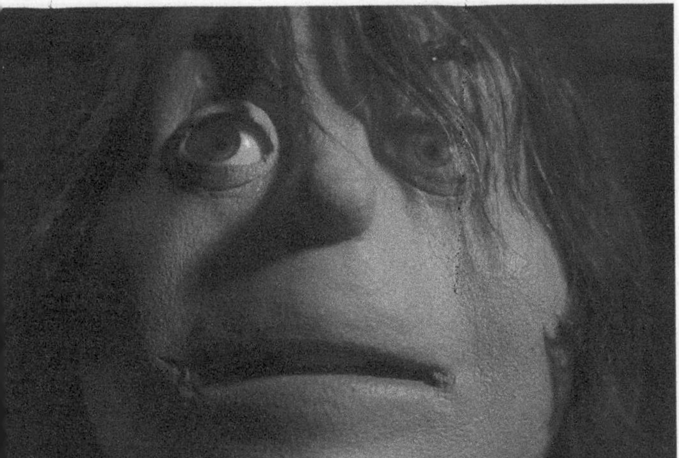

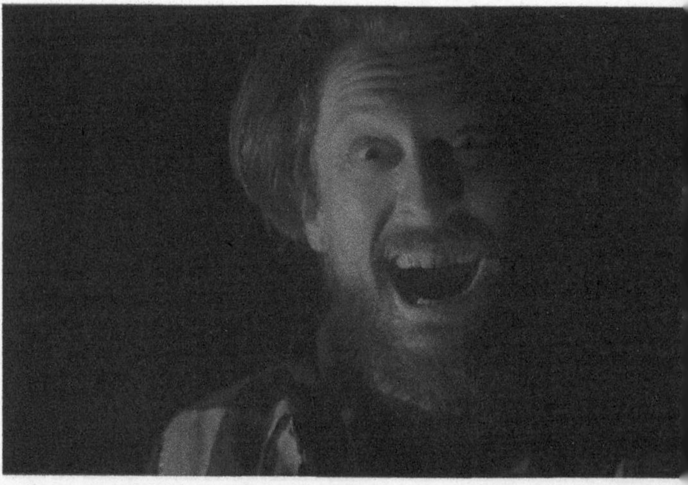

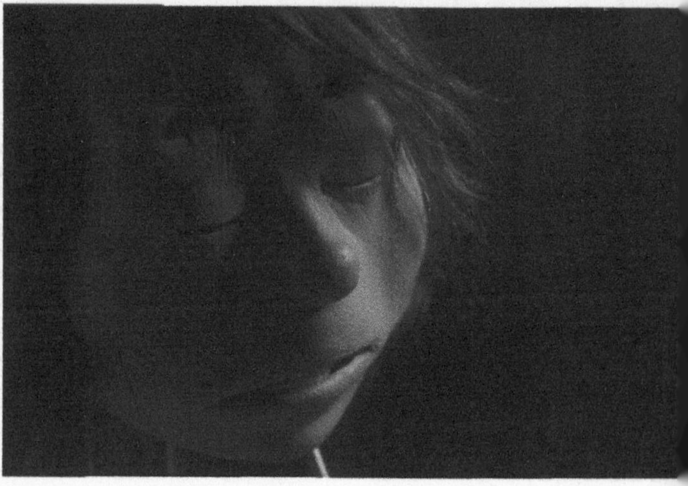

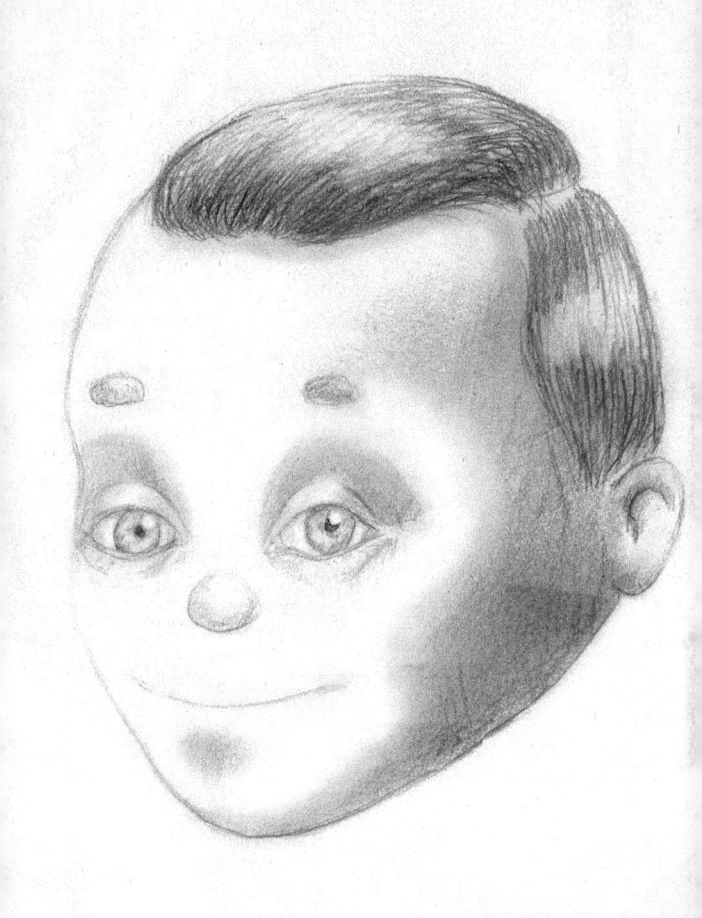

CFX/Life Cycle
Vetro Head Draft 3

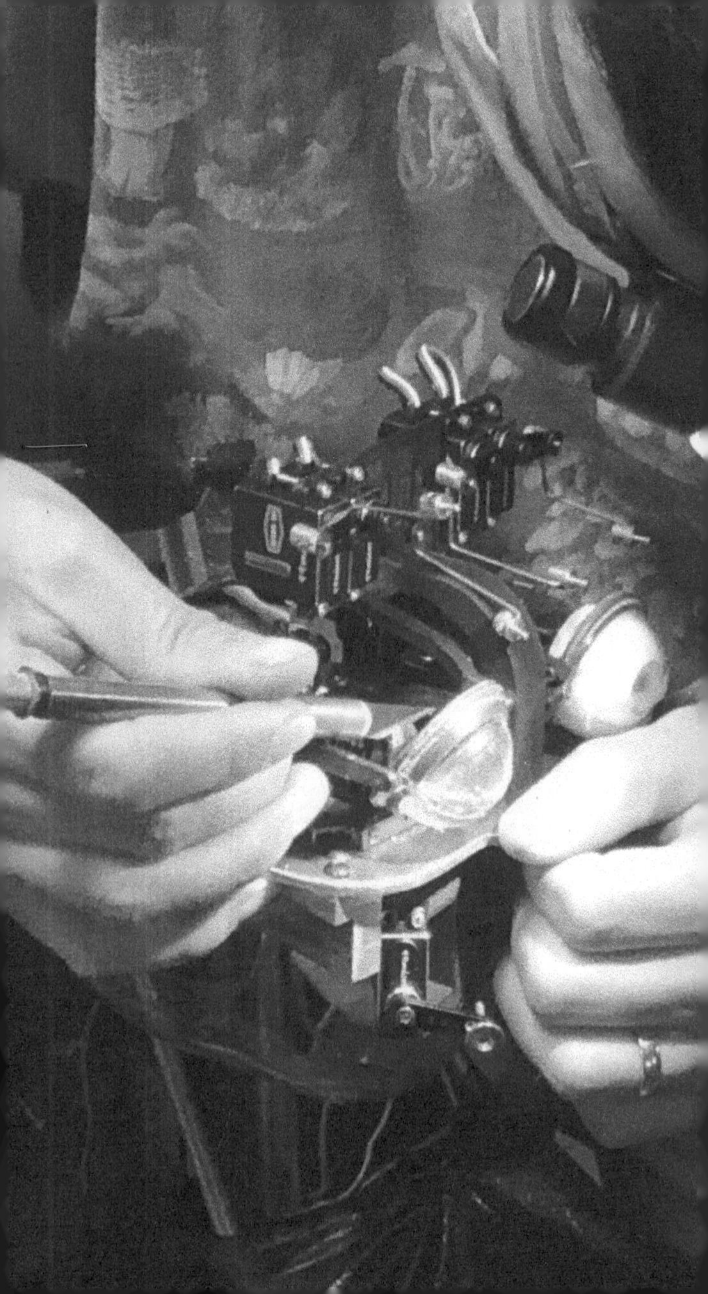

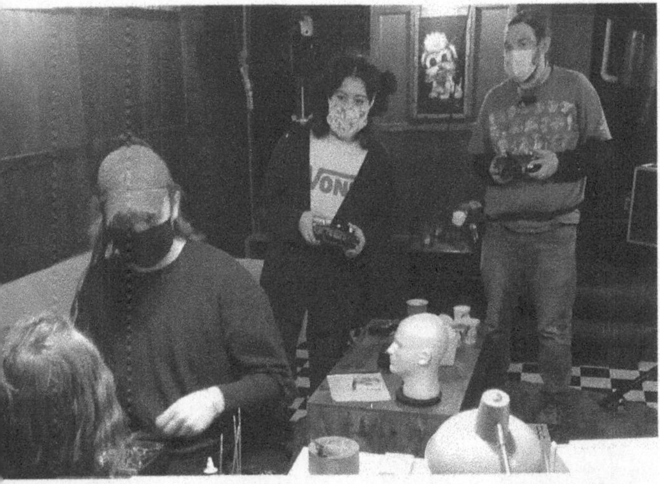

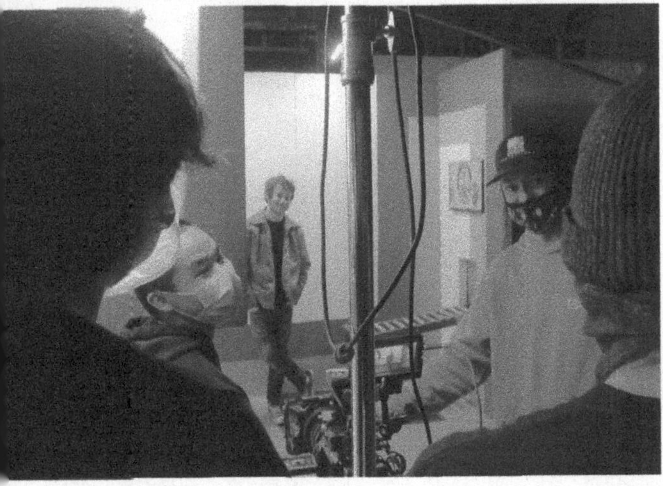

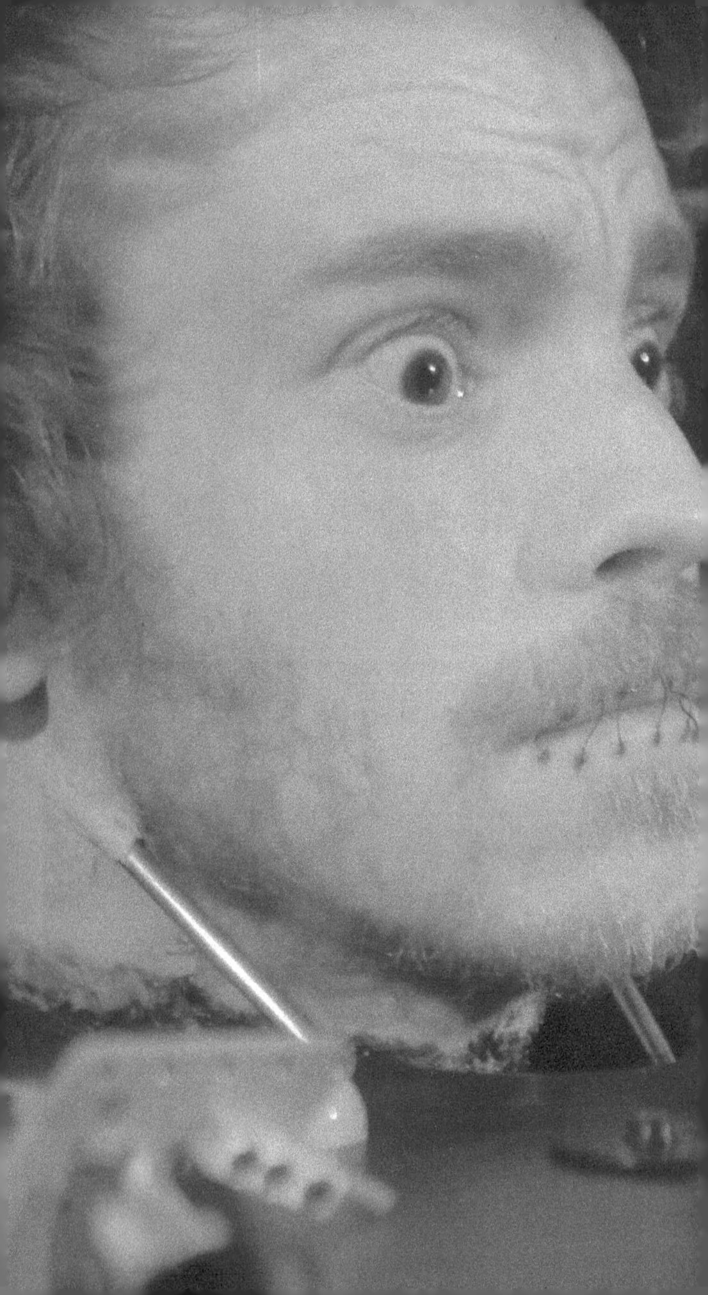

The following pages include Christopher Morvant's adaptation of his short film NIGHT DRIVE. The script was written in 2017 and filmed over three days in a duvetyne covered garage using rear projection and poor man's process to create the driving effect.

It was written as a reflection on personal experiences and as the initial step in the pursuit of a career in film production.

> This film is about dealing with the grief one experiences after having lost someone. I want to connect with the audience on a visceral level in ways in which words alone cannot accomplish.

WRITER/DIRECTOR CHRISTOPHER MORVANT

NIGHT DRIVE

a short story by
CHRISTOPHER MORVANT
based on
his short film

NIGHT DRIVE

Nothing in life or death is easy.

From the dark ashes of the asphalt street rose a white '79 Pontiac Firebird, its luster transitioning from an orange glow to a blue luminescence as the dusk faded in retreat from the impending darkness. In the passenger seat grinned a shadowy figure through an open window.

I stood staring atop the steps that lead from the front door of my childhood home to the street below. I hadn't set foot there in years. Funny how the house looked exactly as I remembered it, yet not as I knew it was.

Regardless, it emanated a warmth in which I longed to remain.

My being ached at the unsettling path before me. It took all my strength to drag my leaden feet forward, down the daunting descent, step by step. Each concrete platform grew longer than the last. The closer I approached, the further I remained.

As it began to seem obvious that I would never reach my destination, there I was, standing beside the driver's door of the glorious Firebird. I opened the door and was punched in the face with nostalgia. I humbly entered the majestic automobile, it was more memory than machine. I knew that smell of the ruby red leather, the firm grip of the steering wheel, the precise tension of each pedal. I felt a beautiful sadness sitting in the elegant Firebird once again.

As I sat meditating, I could feel the passenger's eyes piercing through the calm.

"Are you going to say something or are you going to just sit there and pretend I don't exist?", he questioned from the darkness.

I had no response, only the desire for him to be gone.

His red leather jacket creaked as he leaned over and spoke softly, but accusingly, in my ear, "You have to deal with this eventually."

I knew that voice well but I couldn't place it, a memory of a memory.

I surrendered to the situation and looked over at his coy grin. I saw a face more familiar than my own and yet foreign to my current comprehension, its meaning too distant to distinguish.

I turned the key triggering the raucous roar of the 8 cylinder ignition. The fierce Firebird vibrated with anticipation, her potential power aching to be released. The feeling was a haunting reminder of all the beautiful things I've had and lost. I fought my nihilistic urge to unfurl all of her might and blast forward into certain oblivion, instead gingerly carrying her from first to second, cruising melancholy down the dimly lit suburban street.

The wind howled, the tires sizzled. The Firebird purred, the passenger spoke, "And thus begins the night, extinguishing the day, and with it, all of the shadows light brings."

NIGHT DRIVE

His words echoed in my head before he spoke them. "The shadows, shelter from the lights failed attempt to expose reality. The true face of reality is revealed at night; all will be judged equally in the darkness."

We continued down the deserted suburban landscape through uniform rows of solemn houses watching us with glowing windowed eyes.

The passenger interrogated me, "Could you save them? Would you save them? Is there anything worth saving?"

He fought back a boiling rage behind his intense eyes as he glared back at the leering houses.

"I see signs of life, but no life, as if God himself, bored with the antics of his creation, just flipped a switch and turned them all off."

He had the ferocity of a crazed lunatic. I felt that if I got too close I would be engulfed by the energy he radiated.

"How is it possible to feel so lonely in such a crowded place?"

His temperament heated beyond his ability to contain it, culminating in the explosion of his upper torso out of the open side window in unison with the exclamation, "Are we the only humans left alive!?"

The winter air cooled him enough to allow his steamy form to condensate back into the vehicle. He chuckled while he cranked the window closed, quelling the howling wind.

"We've known each other for almost two decades. I can take one look at your face and know exactly what you're thinking."

He smiled smugly.

"You hate that you have to do this." He speared in and spoke pointedly.

"And you hate me for putting you through this."

The narrow suburban stream was abruptly overtaken by a mighty city river, its banks inundated with the neon lights of bars, liquor stores and motels. Cheap beer, lottery tickets, free HBO and hourly rates. Each block seemed so familiar, each block was indistinguishable from the rest.

A gentle rain showered the car with fine beads that distorted and exaggerated the pageant of illumination. The passenger gazed dreamily at the passing neon blur through the misty window. The vibrance in his face had faded slightly, his eyes had grown foggy and distant.

He seemed to blur into the flowing barrage of light. I felt as though he might dissolve completely without a trace. My stomach ached with guilt at my satisfaction with the idea of wiping him from my memories and being free from this burden.

He arduously pulled himself back from oblivion and spoke with an increasing agitation, "We're victims of our heritage, victims of evolution. Those fine tuned traits that allowed us to thrive in the jungle now haunt and torment us, keeping us apart, alone. Never able to trust one another; always ready in the back of our mind to pounce."

The rapid fluctuation of light intensified as he grew uncontrollably frantic, searching in vain for an escape while shrieking, "Fight or flight! Fight or flight! Fight or flight!"

NIGHT DRIVE

His panic was quashed by a look of inescapable realization. He sobbed softly with a sickly sorrow somewhere between anger and acceptance.

The raindrops tapped the windshield with a hypnotic rhythm. The tires fizzed along the wet road. The city lights danced around the car's interior.

The passenger straightened himself and expanded his chest with a willful inhalation and then fell back with a long defeated exhalation.

He composed himself and stared grievously at me. "I'll tell you what I especially loathe."

His eyes narrowed in disgust. "The beauty of it all."

He returned his longing gaze to the passing procession of pinks, yellows, violets, and blues.

"Because it approaches so near perfection, but fails to reach it. It frustrates me to my core. They say that the meek shall inherit the earth? I say let 'em have it."

He waved his hands with indifference and creaked back in the seat to sulk.

The last city remnants thinned for a few blocks and then finally died with a whimper leaving an endless sand covered horizon of flowing hills. The rain cleared revealing a blood red moon which bathed the world in scarlet.

A hissing sound emanated from the sandy road sliding beneath my tires as we drove down the two lane stretch of highway through the solitary desert.

The passenger's face was a sickly gray, his eyes red with the reflection of the sanguine moon. His disposition was brooding.

The last remnants of humanity passed in the form of massive billboards promising an inevitable infestation. A future of family, swimming pools and barbecues. Don't believe your lying eyes, if you lived here you'd be home by now.

The passenger spoke to me, "Look around you at the infinite space, a landscape of opportunities."

The passenger spoke for me, "But it's just the illusion of possibility. There's nothing you can do to change the path you're trapped on now. Just keep driving and hope you can make it past all these empty promises."

Without warning, he began to laugh uncontrollably. I couldn't help but join him. The absurdity had become too great, the mental toil too cumbersome. Our eyes teared with the joy of a temporary lapse of sanity, freed from the constraints of reality.

As our laughter subsided I felt a brief sense of tranquility. I appreciated the calm stoicism of the infinite desert.

The passenger momentarily mused, "There's something uniquely ethereal about driving the open road: relaxing, soothing. The rhythm, the constant relative motion. Distracting the rational mind with the minutiae of vehicular operations. Numbing that part of the brain that cries out to be occupied, so we can think, unencumbered thought. Tapping into that event horizon where the conscious meets the subconscious."

In the distance rose a seemingly impenetrable wall of mountainous rock. We drove undaunted towards it.

"I wonder if this feeling will exist in the not so distant future, when we're chauffeured along by artificial intelligences. The creators replaced by their creations. The dead gods of a lost civilization. As one zeitgeist swallows its predecessor and is then swallowed, ad infinitum."

The passenger broke down, slamming his fists on the window and crying out in hopeless desperation, "How dare you abandon me!" He curled himself into his own arms and shook softly.

We approached the towering barricade of stone which revealed to us a carved crevice through which a winding road waited to carry us forward.

The passenger's pallor had grown more pale. His gaunt face wore a sense of wonder as he leaned forward and gazed up to appreciate the red and purple rocks jutting up to the heavens.

He pondered aloud, "Look at the sheer magnitude of it. The undeniable order of the jagged chaos towering above us. As though god slammed his fist down in a fit of rage, leaving this beautiful scar on the earth's visage."

He slumped back, his body languishing beneath the weight of the insurmountable landscape. He looked at me with repentance.

"And here we are, two ants scurrying across the desert in search of some crumb of truth; anything to sustain us another day."

He looked at himself with despair.

"But nothing is real, it's only what you perceive it to be; a false memory the instant it occurs."

The moon faded, the stars disappeared into

blackness. Small patches of white began to adorn the headlamp-lit roadside. Flakes of frost gently peppered the windshield, melting on contact. The barrage quickly grew into a flurry that enveloped the car in an impenetrable shroud. The road vanished under a uniform glaze. The Firebird continued forward on instinct alone.

The passenger's complexion matched the blanket of dim white flakes surrounding the car. His body had withered and shrunk into the ruby seat, his red leather jacket becoming indistinguishable from the upholstery: there was no clear line between man and machine.

His breath hung heavy in the air as he struggled to speak.

"You think you could have done something, made a difference?"

I considered responding. I didn't. He did. "What is always was, and what will be already is.

We're all just a measurable mixture of chemicals reacting in a petri dish. There aren't actually possibilities, variables. That's just the illusion. With enough time you could calculate every outcome without variation. This road always has and always will lead here. You're alive, and I'm dead."

The streams of snow evaporated into a thick fog, obscuring all vision. Devoid of any visual frame of reference, I had the distinct sensation that we were drifting through the vacuum of space. I cautiously released pressure from the gas pedal and eased on the brakes but was met with no noticeable difference in velocity. I decided to trust the gauges over my own

NIGHT DRIVE

perception, put on the parking break and rotated the key.

Killing the engine left me trapped in an unbearable silence. I looked to my right and found only the ruby red seat. The space that once the passenger had occupied was now filled with emptiness. I was alone, floating in an endless silent void.

I opened the door and stepped out into the darkness. I felt a momentary relief to make contact with a solid surface, snow crunching under my feet. The thick mist cleared to reveal a frosty path lined on both sides by deteriorated headstones planted atop mounds of earth peaking through the snow.

At the end of the path a giant stone cross protruded out of the ground and rose to the heavens. Seated in front was the passenger, his feeble frame propped against it. I walked towards him.

He looked up at me through tired eyes. His flesh was worn and lifeless, its pallor matching the stone behind. His eyes were dim and recessed. His visible vocal cords crackled as he struggled to speak.

"You know that part of you is glad that I'm dead; that you won't have to deal with what I would have become. You saw the cracks forming, the surface starting to crumble. Besides, I'm grateful to be freed from all this. Free from the pain, the confusion, the frustration. Let loose into the ether."

I attempted to speak but the cold air stole the words.

The passenger spoke for me.

"Don't say a word. Anything you could possibly say would mean less than saying nothing at all. Just get the fuck out of here, drive as fast as you can, and don't look back."

The sky glowed violet in anticipation of the sun's arrival. The fog cleared, the snow melted to reveal the vibrant green grass below.

The passenger was gone, a forgotten dream.

Possibility beyond the scope of capability. What was will never be again.

Nothing in life or death is easy.

NIGHT DRIVE
FILM NOTES

SYNOPSIS:

Otto reluctantly crawls into a '79 Firebird alongside his old friend Perso. Through the suburbs, city, and desert, Perso prods and goads Otto forward along the drive slowly revealing the underlying truths of their relationship and the dark purpose of their journey.

PRODUCTION:

Night Drive was filmed over three days in a duvetyne covered garage using rear projection and poor man's process to create the driving effect.

The original story was written in 2017 as a reflection on personal experiences and as the initial step in the pursuit of a career in film production.

DIRECTOR'S STATEMENT:

This film is about dealing with the grief one experiences after having lost someone. I want to connect with the audience on a visceral level in ways in which words alone cannot accomplish.

FILM NOTES

CAST AND CREW

WRITER/DIRECTOR

Chris Morvant

CAST

Otto: Kory Karam
Perso: Mikael Mattsson

CREW

Produced by: Julian Chisholm
Music by: Noah Ehler
Editor: Chris Morvant
Director of Photography: Tim Le
1st AC: Spencer Wood
2nd AC: Jake Bowren
Production Designer: Tania Peredo
Costume Designer: Connor Fitzgerald
1st AD: Joeli Schwartz
2nd AD: Michael Stevenson
Script Supervisor: Mona Ebrahim
Set PA: Dakota Sedger, Justin Sivilla, Jacob Shapiro
Gaffer: Donavyn Suffel
Best Boy Electric: Byron Morse
Key Grip: Brody Bogert
Best Boy Grip: Hasan Maqsood
Grip: Solomon Rurup, Vasiliy Bondarchuk
Sound Mixer: Milad Salari
Boom Operator: Jacob Woldridge

FILM NOTES

Sound Designer: Chris Morvant
Key Makeup Artist: Ash Rodriguez
Makeup Artist Assistant: Natalie Cooper, Megan Singer
Colorist: Tim Le
Driver: Alex Harris

Scan the QR code to watch NIGHT DRIVE

The following pages include various images from the short film film, Night Drive.

Used by Permission.

The following essays include images from the short film *Night Drive*.

Used by Permission

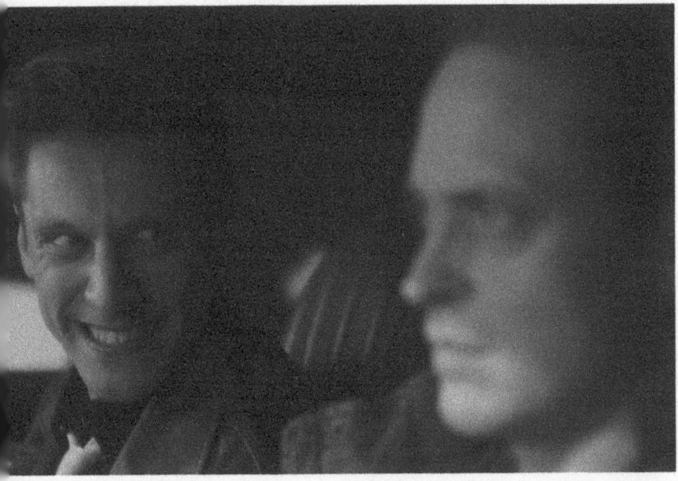

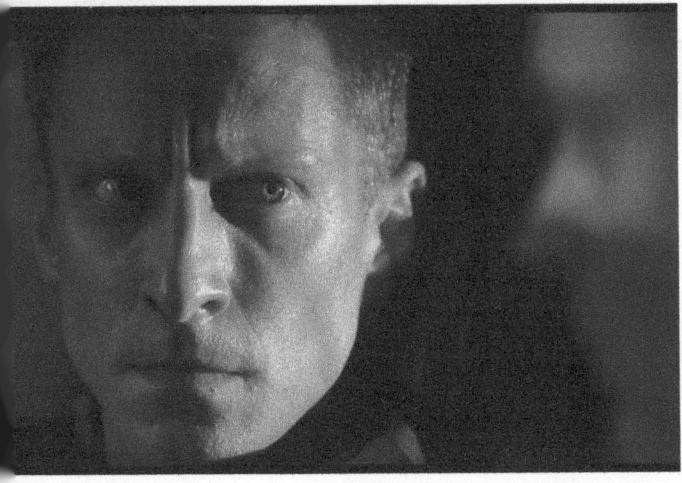

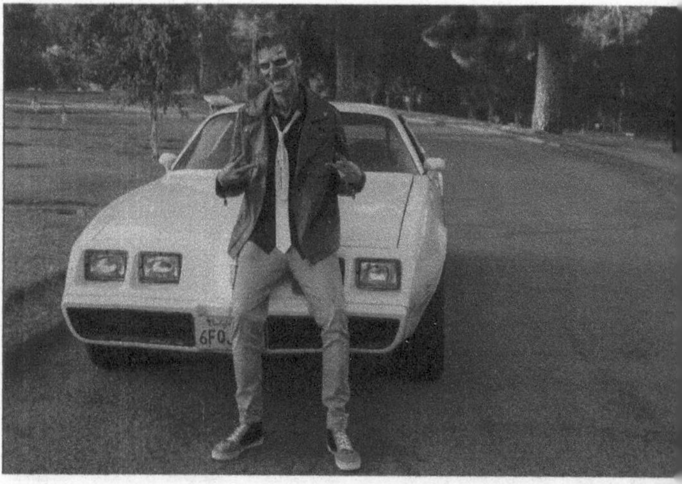

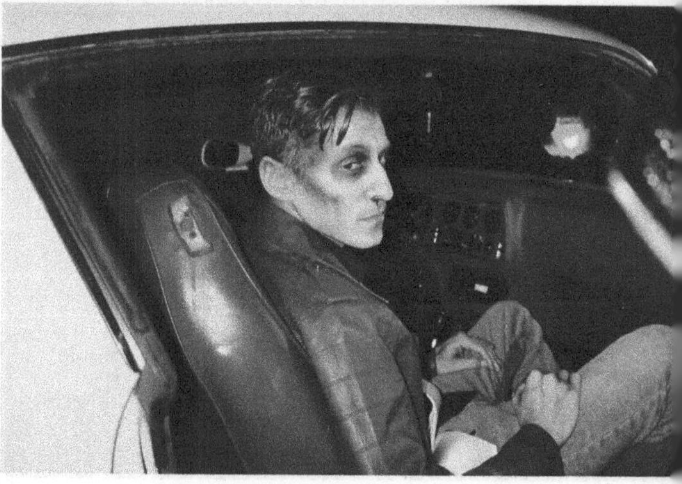

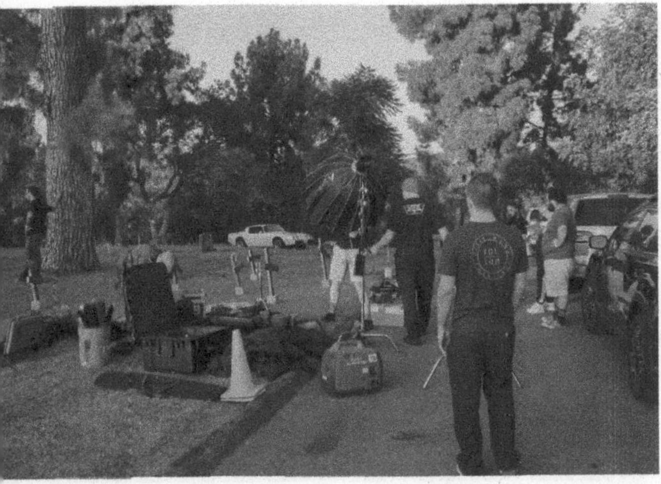

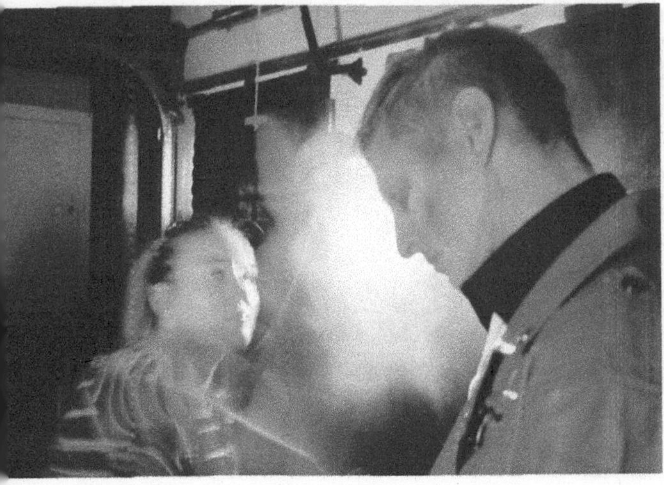

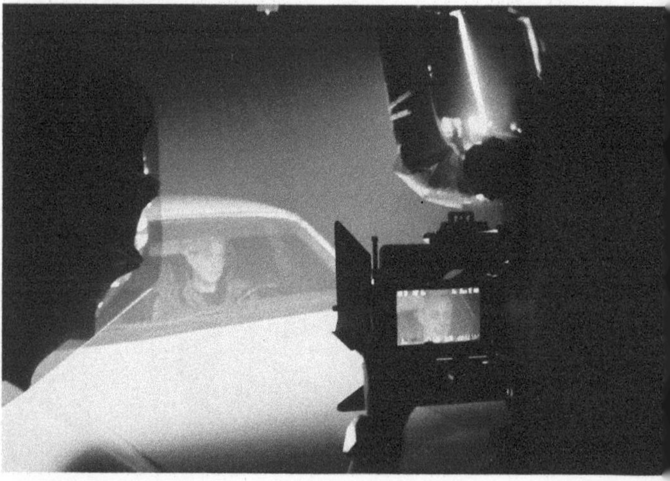

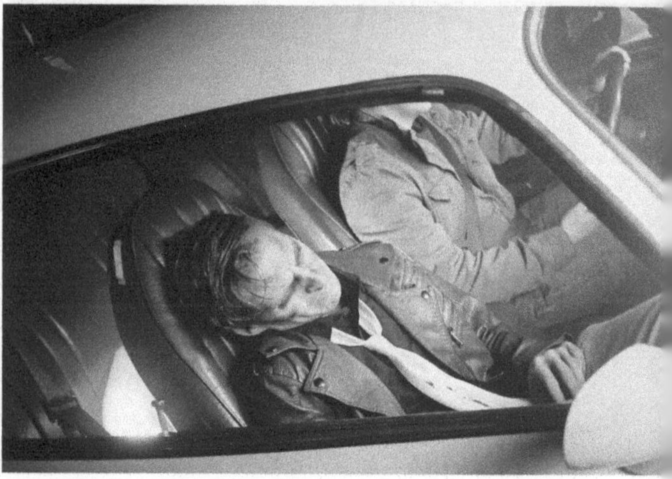

ABOUT THE AUTHOR

Christopher Morvant studied film production at Saddleback College where he wrote and directed four short films. His areas of interest tend towards the surreal with a strong emphasis on internal drama and personal conflict.

NIGHT DRIVE is one of many short films, LIFE CYCLE is his first feature film.

Milton Keynes UK
Ingram Content Group UK Ltd.
UKHW022322011224
451695UK00007B/47